A GAME APART

The real story behind the World Cup in South Africa, 2010

Neal Collins

authorHOUSE®

AuthorHouse™ UK Ltd.
500 Avebury Boulevard
Central Milton Keynes, MK9 2BE
www.authorhouse.co.uk
Phone: 08001974150

© *2010 Neal Collins. All rights reserved.*

No part of this book may be reproduced, stored in a retrieval system, or transmitted by any means without the written permission of the author.

First published by AuthorHouse 1/11/2010

ISBN: 978-1-4490-5747-3 (sc)
ISBN: 978-1-4490-5748-0 (hc)

This book is printed on acid-free paper.

DEDICATION

To my wife Tracy, who read every word. And to my mum, who put up with my leftie nonsense but never got to read the book.

FOREWORD /PREFACE/ INTRODUCTION

I was approached in September 2009 by a literary agent who asked, given my background (see profile below) if I had any great ideas for a World Cup book, given the greatest football tournament on earth will take place in Africa for the first time soon, kicking off in Johannesburg on June 11, 2010.

I had just got in from a glorious night at Wembley Stadium, where I saw England thump Croatia 5-1 with my three sons and 93,000 like-minded people to qualify for the finals, which will stir the sports world and, hopefully, the real world too.

I considered a few factual ideas but then decided a fictional account of how South Africa as a football nation has developed since the dark days of Apartheid when I lived there in the 1980s, taking the reader through to the dawn of democracy in 1993 and the big kick-off at Soccer City, 2010.

I developed a structure for the book while on a flight to South Africa to watch cricket's Champions Trophy (via Tripoli of all places) in October 2009 and tried desperately to come up with a suitable title for a book so with such far-reaching erm... goals.

A GAME APART is based largely on what I witnessed myself as a student, footballer and very junior sports journalist from 1979 to 1985. The only major incident I did not witness is the Trojan Horse massacre - but a similar atrocity is well-documented as having taken place in Athlone, near Cape Town in 1985.

Since leaving the country – as a conscientious objector, I received a hand-written call up to attend National Service for June 1985 despite my British citizenship - I have made numerous return visits to South Africa to cover the Lions rugby tour (1997), the cricket World Cup (2003) as well as a three-month England cricket tour (1999/2000). My father still lives there and we visit, as a family, at least once a year, travelling widely and without fear other than when we come across big cats and rogue elephants in the game parks.

These frequent trips have, I hope, given me a special insight into a fascinating nation, so unique in Africa... and the world, when you consider how quickly it has changed.

In all my years resident there from 1970 to 1985, and on over two dozen subsequent visits, I never been mugged or car-jacked, or even rudely spoken to by a black man, though my university days were marked by constant conflict with the police, which reflects itself in what you find below.

The events detailed in the book are largely factual, but condensed... names and places have been altered, some may feel they recognise themselves in certain of the characters, but in truth the characters are a compilation of the people I have met, the life I experienced. I judge nobody who lived in South Africa at that time, where so many were forced into certain roles by the incredible pressures of a violent, divisive society.

A lot of the publicity surrounding the upcoming World Cup has been negative, with the focus on crime and corruption in South Africa since democracy arrived in 1993. My perception is very different to that... I believe the country has changed massively for the better in 16 short years. I've waited all that time to let my memories loose, and the World Cup seems an appropriate time to write a novel that, I hope, will help people to remember exactly what the Rainbow Nation has been through in the last 25 years.

My memories, my distortions in terms of time and emphasis, will annoy some, please others. All I ask is that the reader recognises this is how a young Englishman might have viewed the South Africa I grew up in. A strange but beautiful country riven by cruelty and mistrust and headed for a bloody revolution… until the release of a certain Nelson Mandela in 1990. That South Africa is now in a position to bid for a major sports event, let alone host an operation of this scale, is little short of a miracle given what I lived through there. And that really is the point. For those who visit the country, for those who view it on a television screen, for those who read about it in the newspapers, I hope to offer some perspective. Apartheid, like the Holocaust, should never be forgotten, swept under the carpet. Otherwise somebody will simply repeat the process. And that must never be allowed to happen.

ACKNOWLEDGMENTS

NEAL COLLINS is a sport journalist based in London. He makes regular appearances as a football and sports analyst on Channel 5 and Sky News. Born in Plymouth (01/03/1961) but raised in Lee on Solent, Hampshire, Collins spent his formative years in South Africa, after emigrating with his parents in 1970. After winning a series of essay awards at Lyttelton Manor High School in Centurion, Collins won a scholarship to and then graduated from Rhodes University, Grahamstown with a Bachelor of Journalism degree. He also majored in sociology and worked during his vacations at the Rand Daily Mail, a liberal South African paper now sadly closed. Collins played football for Durban City, South Africa's league champions in 1981 and 1982 but never graduated beyond the reserve team after being coached by current Fulham manager Roy Hodgson at his junior club, Berea Park in Pretoria. He played cricket for Villagers, a first grade club in Pretoria. Though chiefly a sports journalist, Collins frequently wrote articles which upset the Apartheid Government in the early 1980s while working for the Natal Mercury and Daily News newspapers in Durban and, when he received a hand-written call-up for two years of National Service despite his English passport in 1985, he returned to England. After a year on the Buckinghamshire Advertiser when he was commended in the Sports Council's annual journalism awards, he joined the Today newspaper launched by Eddie Shah in 1986. In 1990 he moved to the Sunday Mirror as Assistant Sports Editor. He joined the Daily Mail as Assistant Sports Editor in 2000 after attending the Sydney Olympics for the Mirror Group. Collins then joined the Sunday People in 2002, covering rugby and cricket as well as performing the role of Sports News Editor. He followed the build-up and eventual triumph of Sir Clive Woodward's England rugby team in Sydney in 2003. He joined the Evening Standard in 2005 and was appointed London Lite Sports Editor in 2006. He lives in Chalfont St Giles, Buckinghamshire with his wife Tracy and four children, twins Kriss and Laura, 21, and Harry, 14, and Charlie, 12. **He is an Arsenal fan and named his first dog Charlie George in 1972.**

PROLOGUE

"Wisdom is like a baobab tree; no one individual can embrace it."
Akan proverb (Benin, Ghana and Togo)

THE Sangoma is there, in the darkest recess of the dressing room. On his haunches. Huge. Silent. Timeless. He's been there all night, protecting their honour, confirming their luck. Praying to a God which is both Roman and African. Or neither. He stands wordlessly as the team enters, heads bowed, scared to look at "Mad-Eyes" Dlamini, their highly-strung witchdoctor. Dlamini ignores them all. And makes straight for the Englishman. Without a word, he lifts Charlie's tee-shirt, muttering, nodding, gyrating... no, he's actually vibrating, and it moves the very air around him. The medicine man takes a long fingernail and slowly draws a line across Charlie's solar plexus. Charlie nearly giggles. Then he looks down and watches, horrified, as a thin line of blood appears where the nail had passed painlessly across his skin. No sign of a knife or a blade... just that thin red line. Reaching back into his huge dark pot, the Sangoma, clad only in an animal skin skirt and a ludicrously bright feathered head-dress, pulls a long ribbon from the bubbling cauldron and ties it around Charlie's midriff. On the surface of the liquid in the calabash, a lady's expensive finger, complete with wedding band and bright red fingernail, floats next to a small animal skull and a tightly coiled millipede. The Sangoma takes his forefinger and trails putrid liquid across the weeping line of blood on his stomach. Charlie's vision begins to fail, his stomach cramps, he is teetering on the edge of a crevasse, he hears bird song. Then the team talk begins...

CHAPTER 1: PRAYING

"Words are like bullets; if they escape, you can't catch them again."
                        Wolof proverb (Senegal, Gambia)

"IT'S not much like Fareham," grunted Charlie, as the dirt-grey minibus careered around the corner on two wheels. Jabu laughed as the Englishman clung on, knuckles white, to his football boots, still crusty with Hampshire mud.

"KwaMashu," Jabu beamed, gesturing expansively at the houses emerging from the bush on the left of the highway, "Home of the urban Zulu. God's own township! Usuthu!"

Charlie was reminded, eerily, of Coronation Street in black and white. Tightly packed rows of houses, ramshackle shacks and tiny brick buildings, rising up the hill in ragged ranks with a pall of smoke hanging over the valley. Hardly any cars, no street lights, no telephone boxes. 1984? This was more like 1904. A huge lurch then, as the singing, laughing taxi driver took his hi-ace off the broad modern motorway straight onto a dirt track barely visible through the bush, avoiding the smooth off-ramp half a mile further on. Charlie prayed quietly.

"Only way to avoid the cops," said Jabu, his belt fighting a losing battle with his Santa Claus stomach as they jolted over the unmade road. "You'll get used to the taxis. Not like London, me old China, this is Durban! Hau!"

Charlie had landed at the untidy little airport, flanked by a dangerous-looking oil refinery and several even-more-dangerous-looking armed policemen, just half-an-hour earlier. For the proffered five rand – about a pound – the taxi drivers had gathered around him, offering to drive him anywhere, anytime. But then Jabu had arrived, picked his trusty man, chosen his rusty ride, and without instruction the first leg of Charlie's safari was underway. Everyone knew Jabu (short for *Jabulani* or *Happiness*), everyone knew where they would be heading.

A huge truck cut across the dirt track, bringing the taxi to a shuddering halt at an informal crossroads. Rising from the sugar cane around them, a gathering of less-than-savoury youths appeared and moved ominously towards them. They carried sticks, wore rags and hungry expressions. One hefted a huge, curved metal sword, a cane-cutting panga. Trouble. Until they spied the corpulent taxi passenger. They dropped their eyes, smiles broke out. As they backed off, Jabu laughed, threw a couple of coins out of the half-opened window, and they were off again.

"You okay?" said Jabu, as they passed a squatter camp perched precariously on the edge of a quarry, children squabbling, juggling a tennis ball yards from a merciless ravine. "It's okay, you won't be living out here, you'll be in that larnie hotel on Marine Parade, just like Bournemouth it is, I've seen the post cards!"

Charlie laughed, clutched his boots. Jabu needed "an English style centre forward" to bang them in. He had tracked down Charles Ivor Burton (23, right-footed, striker, Portsmouth Under 18, released) via a word-of-mouth scouting system and a grainy video cassette. A career-high 32 goals for Fareham in the Southern League last year had put him in modest provincial newspaper headlines; a local scout with a cousin in Durban had posted a couple of home-movie highlights to Jabu... and then he'd had the series of expensive and slightly crazy telephone calls with Jabu, chairman of Chaka Royals, the footballing heart and soul of KwaZulu.

It wasn't quite a foreign move to New York Cosmos or Toronto

White Caps like some of his Pompey mates but hey, three months in South Africa would pay him significantly more than five shifts in the fish and chip shop and the £30-a-game-tucked-in-the-boots he was earning at the moment. And the pound-rand exchange rate was getting better by the day.

Mission-educated Jabu Samuel Ntulani was a big man in all ways. An enthusiastic part of the process which had brought together the all-white National Football League, the black National Professional Soccer League and most of the Asian Soccer Federation six years before, Jabu had ploughed all his resources into the Chaka Royals, legitimising his chain of illegal shebeens, brothels and protection rackets to create a powerhouse in the barrier-breaking, newly-founded National Professional League.

Jabu's great-great-grand-father, so legend had it, had fought with courage alongside Chaka, the great Zulu King, against the Boers and the British and anybody else who fancied an assegai where it hurts. Creating a football team to crush the traditional white clubs, the fancy Asian hopefuls and the Sowetan giants had become his overwhelming ambition in a nation where football – along with, perhaps, jazz music and boxing – provided a rare avenue to public acclaim for the disenfranchised majority of the population.

Jabu smiled at his new signing: tall, slim, tough-looking... "good in the air, nice touch, great nose for goals" is what his spies, expensively packaged off to England, had told him. Charlie's goals had taken Fareham to the top of the Southern League, the second round proper in the great FA Cup... and he'd even scored a hat-trick against Oxford – City, not United, but who was counting?

Some of the clubs had gone for the big-time English pros. Derek Dougan had come out to play for Arcadia in Pretoria and taken Peter Withe back with him, Geoff Hurst had appeared for Cape Town City and won over 40 penalties in one season, changing the face of penalty area challenges forever. The list was endless. Bobby Moore, Gordon Banks, Francis Lee, Ian St John.... All had trodden the path Charlie was now embarking upon.

But, a voracious reader of the football magazines and a networker *par excellance*, Jabu knew the problems.

Durban City, the local "white" club had experienced all sorts of trouble with their glamour signings. The homesickness, the phone calls home, the endless struggle to convince a top First Division player from Southampton or Stoke it was worth spending his summers travelling 400 miles from tropical, lush Durban to dry, high altitude Johannesburg most weekends, or to wet, windy Cape Town nearly 1,000 miles around the coast.

So he'd gone for the cut-price option. Low-risk, high-return. The tough young British pro from the lower echelons of football. It had worked with Withe. He'd been at Southport and Barrow before emigrating to Port Elizabeth City and Arcadia Shepherds. From there, he had returned to Nottingham Forest and Aston Villa, winning two First Division Championship and a European Cup. Who would have predicted that?

This man Burton would be perfect. Cheap, cheerful… and "with a nose for goal". He loved the phrase. Jabu wrinkled his not-insubstantial nose. He had plenty of talented players, thousands of hungry lads waiting in the wings. And a couple of hulking great defenders who could stop tanks. But goal-scorers anywhere in the world are a rare commodity. And Jabu knew that. Like he knew most things. Instinctively. In his not-insubstantial gut.

Into the township proper now, and it was like nothing Charlie had seen before, even in Greece on holiday. Stray dogs, stray children. Rubbish blowing, sirens screaming. And that smell…it was Charlie's turn to wrinkle his nose now. "Tear gas," growled Jabu, "Been a bit of trouble, couple of funerals. The hostage siege at the consulate went wrong last week."

"Saw it on the news," said Charlie, "I didn't realise it happened near here."

"About five miles that way," said Jabu, as a police helicopter flew low overhead and an armoured car stalked across the road ahead. "Our people were protesting outside and the cops just cleared the road. Said it was impeding the shoppers, an illegal gathering. Five dead, 70 injured, just another day in paradise…"

"Hey, look, I'm with you guys…" Charlie started. "Apartheid, Steve Biko, Martin Luther King, Mahatma Ghandi, Nelson Man…"

"Stop," said Jabu, the beam fading for the first time in their 45-minute relationship. "Black men don't talk politics with white men in South Africa, Charlie. Not since the Afrikaners took over after the war. Here, you're just a footballer. You bang the goals in. That's what I'm paying you for, that's what you do. If you score a bloody hat-trick against Chiefs or Pirates and they all want to interview you, you talk football, never mention Apartheid, don't you dare. Or you'll end up banned. Under house arrest. Or disappeared. Seriously. Never seen again."

Charlie nodded. This wasn't the time to argue. He had views. He'd seen changes in Britain that pleased him. God, at school they'd called him black because of his dark curly hair and permanent tan. He'd pointed to Paul Reaney of Leeds and England, not to mention Mike Trebilcock, Everton's FA Cup winning hero in 1966. Argument over, though mum did say she thought his dad had come from Trinidad… but what did that matter? She was mostly tipsy these days anyway, could barely remember beyond yesterday. Ah mum…

Tears. The gas was stinging his eyes, his mouth, under his arms where he was sweating slightly, even in the middle of a Natal winter. "Understood," he said, "Not my business… but it pisses me off what they did to Basil D'Oliviera."

Dolly was the Cape "coloured" cricketer who had been forced to go to Worcestershire to pursue his career as a highly effective all-rounder. He'd ended up being too good to leave out of the England side to tour South Africa – despite clandestine attempts to keep him out of the squad – and the South African president BJ Vorster had refused to allow the MCC to tour in 1968. That had led to the start of the international sports boycott.

Even now, South Africa were under FIFA suspension and world football's governing body took a dim view of players who came to end their careers in South Africa. Tony Kay and Peter Swan, the Sheffield Wednesday players banned in the match-fixing scandal of 1962, had come out. And Arno Steffenhagen and Volkmar Gross, who were among the 70 Germans caught in a similar scandal some years later, emigrated for footballing winters in substantial numbers.

With Peter Hain, the activist who would one day become a high-ranking Labour politician in England, leading the opposition, South African sport had been reduced to inviting "rebel" cricket teams and "superstar" football teams to play them, though curiously, rugby's Lions generally managed to turn up for an official ding-dong every few years. Rugby was a religion for the Afrikaners, football was the Englishman's game, though both sports had originated on the public school fields of the old colony-basher.

Charlie was rare among his footballing colleagues. He thought the South Africans deserved isolation for what they had done to Dolly and the others like him. Talented sportsmen restricted just because they were black – or in Dolly's case, slightly off-white.

Then there was Soweto in 1976. What they called the "School's Uprising". He'd seen the riots, the violence, the whole thing on telly. Charlie read the papers, watched the news. He knew a bit. He wasn't thick. He'd only left school early because of the taunts, the bullies…and the need to kick a ball for a living.

"Seriously Jabu, it's all wrong.." he began.

"Ah, you English," laughed Jabu, "So bloody liberal when you get here. Give the old servant an extra fiver… pat her chocolate-button baby on the head… and then vote for the National Party when the election comes along. Doesn't take you long.

"It's the same with all the Europeans. Come over here and say they aren't racist. Then they see how they can live in Africa; the Poles, the Greeks, the Lebanese, the Brits… and all those Germans after the war. And they change real quick. European emigrants bolster the political system here, while their governments back home talk out against Apartheid.

"I've never worked it out. So liberal at home, so conservative the minute they set foot in Africa.

"There'll be problems in your country too one day if people don't change the way they think. Anyway, why are you so dark, didn't look that way on the video."

"Bloody cheap camera," said Charlie, slightly embarrassed, "Mum thinks dad was from Jamaica, she's not sure."

Jabu laughed: "Don't tell the authorities that, they'll make you live in KwaMashu! Just stay British my friend, it's easier that way. Ah, here it is… our Zulu Highbury!"

They turned, on two wheels as ever, into a narrow gateway emblazoned "Princess Magogo Stadium", a once-grand edifice which was starting to crumble slightly at the edges. About 300 locals, varying from the well-dressed to the tribal, stood in a knot in the car park.

They began chanting as the mini-bus approached. "Usuthu," they rumbled, "Usuthu" the old Zulu war cry which had struck fear into generations of English soldiers. Charlie felt it. Goose bumps. Michael Caine. Things moving deep inside him. But then the beaming smiles broke out around him as he clambered out of the sliding door, boots still firmly in hand, to greet what looked like his first tiny band of autograph hunters.

Only they didn't want his signature. One was trying to clip a bit of hair, another had twisted the button off his coat quicker than a Gerd Muller turn.

Charlie drew back: "What...?" Jabu smiled: "They want your magic, your muti. Just a little something they can keep to bring you luck."

Without time to consider his various miniscule losses, Charlie found himself confronted by his first white face, a short, chubby man with the look of a former footballer... short, bandy-legged, red-nosed... and very, very Geordie.

"Haway lad," he said, proffering a hand, "Clive Fox, me brother John played for Sunderland..."

"Yeah, Johnny Fox, seen him on Match of the Day," said Charlie, "Good to meet you..."

"Just call me gaffer," said Clive, "I'm the boss here... after Jabu of course."

Jabu smiled with a paternal air, waved away the mob and guided them to the doors of the stadium. "In there lad, kit on," said Clive, throwing him a pair of shorts and a training shirt in Royals green colours, "We'll see you out there."

The dressing room too, was a long, long way from Fareham. Drab, unpainted, dirty. And the smell! Cinnamon... tobacco... cannabis... urine... and something... blood?

The door opened as he changed. A huge African man filled the doorway. Too heavy to be a footballer, too old, too lined, he spoke in a low, resonant voice: "Charles," he said, "It's good to see you..."

"Sabona," said Charlie, trying out the only word of Zulu he knew, taught in 13 hours on the flight from Heathrow. It was just about the only thing he got out of the PR girl from Pietermaritzburg. "I see you," the big man responded, "I'm the captain here, Mlungisi Malekane... but you can just call me Professor. I will be your guide, Englishman. Trust me."

Instantly, the conversation became surreal, almost magical. As he spoke, the huge man in the doorway seemed to give out more than words. The Professor's conversation was like heavy syrup, drifting slowly through the air towards him, delicious reassurance, sweet platitudes. Charlie shook his head, trying to find reality somewhere in this tiny room in the middle of an African township. It wouldn't come. Must be jet lag. Time stretched, bent, distended. But he felt good inside, happy for the first time since the airport and that bloody taxi. The Professor said: "There will be trials but you will come through them, trust me," and then, curiously "Your father was from Alabama..." or Charlie may just have imagined it.

Then he was trotting out behind the Professor, in full kit, ready to join what looked like a reasonably regimented shooting exercise. Gathered behind the goal there must have been a thousand green-clad Royals fans, clapping politely when the goals went in.

The surface was not quite Fratton Park. Wembley after the Royal Horseshow in 1970 perhaps. Bobbling, rough, his first two shots flew wide; the rest of the team, all black, skinny – apart from the Prof – and very quiet while Clive barked his orders, looked at him with something approaching pity.

Then the coach's pass rolled true, he caught the ball with ankle locked, knee cocked, and bang, Henry the goalkeeper was left to watch and admire. Confidence surged. Goals came. Henry's gloves – which looked suspiciously like they were made for the garden - were suitably stung. Football, Charlie's lifeblood, was flowing through his veins.

Crosses next. The Prof was putting them in. Not like a good old English semi-pro winger. Full of tricks and feints. Once or twice he put his right foot around the back of his left and produced inch perfect balls with the most ridiculous ease. None of the lads could really head, they barely challenged as Charlie rose, salmon like, and peppered the goal with powerful headers.

Clive shouted: "Merv, Andy! Here, up!"

Two big white guys got up from the back of the stands, putting out cigarettes and trying to look cool as they removed shades and smiled at the fans. One was plainly South African, moustache, blond hair, tall, looked like one of those Springbok rugby players. The other, plainly, was an enormous Scot. "Hi, I'm Andy McGeechan, my brother Pat played for Hibs," he said, "I'm the captain."

Hmm. Two captains. One full of mystique and mastery, the other dominant in the air, teak-tough on the floor. Ebony and Ivory. And they barely exchanged a word through a five-a-side session which reminded Charlie of pre-season at Fareham, when the Sunday League hopefuls were trying to muscle their way past the regulars for a winter of money-in-the-boots.

Nasty tackles, elbows, shoving, pushing. And then a ridiculous fitness session involving lap after lap, push up after push up… and a gazillion sit-ups. And then a final five-a-side revenge match. Clive goaded them, pushed them, urged confrontation.

Sweat soaked, the session was brought to a halt when Merv clattered the tiny bloke. The fans had been shouting "Ace" whenever he touched the ball. Barely five foot high, he had Wednesday legs as in "Wednesday going to break?" Charlie explained the joke three times. No laughs. Thulani "Ace" Ntsoeleng's ability with the ball was phenomenal, until Merv got hold of him at about thigh height.

A brief melee ensued, a slap, more than what footballers would normally call handbags… Merv started shouting about "Kaffirs" and Clive called it all off, quickly, before things got out of hand.

Merv was assigned to give Charlie a lift into Durban, Jabu left to do a quick tour of his shebeens, "the club still needs money," he explained.

Vusi Nkosi, the right back, skilful but too lightweight to make it anything above non-League in England, wouldn't let it go. Merv hadn't gone near him all night but Vusi was furious over the Ace incident. Even before that, his accusing stare had followed Charlie all day. Now it was Merv's turn. Muttering under the breath, and now, as they prepared to leave in Merv's bakkie – a pick-up in American terms – Vusi was approaching fast.

Charlie knew he was a strange one, at one point he'd said to the Prof: "We don't need the Englishman. Too many whites already." Charlie had heard it. Chose to ignore it. Now Vusi wasn't to be ignored. Though a head shorter than Merv, his right hand shot to the big man's throat. "Kaffirs? Is that what you say? Bad choice Merv..."

Vusi's hand struck like a cobra, a stinging slap to the big man's cheek. Merv swung wildly, then kicked out, but Vusi was away from him, twisting from Andy's grip too. "Jou vokking doner!" screamed Merv in Afrikaans, "You fucking thunder".

This was trouble. Jabu was gone, Clive was nowhere to be seen. Vusi stood three yards back, steaming. Merv smiled slowly. "Come on then Vusi, my little Communist, come to daddy," he said, and charged him.

Vusi tried to dodge but Merv caught him with half a fist on the temple. Vusi staggered and tried to respond with a roundhouse right. It landed square on Merv's jaw. But he just smiled. "South African Defence Force light-heavyweight champion, 1978," he grinned, grabbed Vusi by the collar and drew back a meaty right fist.

While the rest stood and watched, Charlie stepped forward, grabbing the hand. "Hey, I thought I'd come to play for a football team, not a bunch of bloody idiots," he yelled, "Now leave it Merv, he hit you, you hit him, leave it!"

Charlie had a certain presence. More mouth than trouser to be truthful. And, no, he'd never actually had a fist fight. Even when Steve from the prefabs had hit him and stolen his wristwatch in year five. But he couldn't watch that fist hit that face. Not on his first day in Africa.

Merv turned his attention to Charlie, dropping Vusi, swinging fast. "Vokking Rooinek!" he grunted, "I hate the English. You killed 17 of my cousins in the Boer War you..."

Charlie ducked and hit him once, hard, in the stomach. Merv doubled up, catching his head on Charlie's knee. And down he went. Silence. Shit. More silence. Merv stirred.

"Get up Merv," he said with an authority he didn't feel, "This happens all the time in English football. Training ground spats they call them. Get over it. Vusi, shake the man's hand."

Grinning, Vusi stepped forward. As Merv rose to one knee, a gleam came into the little Zulu's eye. "Don't even think about it, Vusi," barked Charlie. Merv rose unsteadily. "Sheez man, you've got a hard fist Charlie!" he grunted, rubbing his chin. The part Charlie's knee had played in his finest, luckiest hour was neatly forgotten.

"Look, forget it guys. I don't know what kaffir means, I don't know why you called him a Communist, but the truth? I just want to play football, not spend the next three months breaking up fights. Now shake, and be done. I need to get my head down."

Surprisingly, they did just that. Merv had developed the national serviceman's ability to accept authority. Vusi had been raised to respect signs of bravery. A strange handshake ensued, with a bit of shaking about and finger tapping, and both men ended up laughing, gently, at their brief conflict.

On the drive back into Durban, Andy McGeechan and Merv van Tonder gave Charlie their "welcome to South Africa" speech. He was warned never to trust the "coons", to take Jabu's money and go back to Durban, to keep out of the shebeens, and "whatever you do, don't socialise with them. We'll show you a good time."

Merv had been plucked out of the local white amateur league two years ago, to bolster the defence and take his 50-yard throw-ins so beloved of the Royals fans. Andy had come to Natal to play for the now-defunct Durban United in the old white NFL and had got a good job in a local bank, beguiling local businessmen with his Edinburgh accent. Now the pair of them formed a much-feared centre-back duo for the Royals, fourth in the NPSL last season.

Other white players had come and gone, unable to settle. Merv was clearly on the verge of doing the same. "Kaffirs, they know nothing," he growled, "I spent two years on the border fighting the Cubans and the gooks on the Caprivi Strip. Even the Cubans don't trust the fucking coons. Sure, they can play football. But they don't like whites on the field. You should hear them boo Robbie de Graaf when he plays for Chiefs. The black guys have all the skill, but they can't tackle. They can't run for 90 minutes. They drink. They smoke shit. They shag anything that moves."

That said, Merv then broke into an autobiographical anecdote which featured his own copious drinking, cheap marijuana and women of dubious repute along Point Road, the dockside red-light district in Durban.

Andy was gentler. "There are educated black guys now. They're letting them into the white universities. And the Asians in Durban are pretty serious. But best you keep to the sea-front and the city. There's a few clubs I can show you. A few women I can introduce you to. You'll love it. Like a holiday for three months. And Jabu pays up just what he promises. Win bonuses in a brown envelope, no tax, no bullshit. Just score the goals and take the money."

They took him to the Edward hotel on the beachfront, checked him in, flirted with the receptionists. The Edward was a huge old Victorian establishment which was, as Jabu had said, not a little redolent of Bournemouth or Brighton. In the lounge, a slightly faded showgirl tonked the piano and sang "Memories" while Merv and Andy continued Charlie's African education.

"It's whites only here," said Andy, "And the beaches are whites only too. Get a lot of tourists from inland. But don't wear expensive watches, they'll take them. And don't leave anything on the beach, it'll go. Get a hired car. The buses are only for the blacks. And never take a train."

By now Charlie was exhausted. Jabu had seemed an intelligent bloke. A level above any of the club chairmen he'd come across in his career. He knew what it was all about. The players had looked pretty good to him. Bit lightweight perhaps. Now Andy and Merv were unravelling any feel-good factor with their stories, their paranoia. If they felt like that about black people, why live in Africa? But he realised that question had been asked by far brighter people than a semi-pro footballer hoping for three months in the sun.

Merv and Andy made their excuses after a half-hearted invite to a club further up Marine Parade "with a British comedian and a stripper, the cops don't know" but Charlie hadn't slept for 24 hours. Day one in South Africa was over. He was knackered. And confused. Sleep came quickly in the opulent double bed, as good as anything he'd ever slept in.

And he thought about that squatter camp, the corrugated iron shacks perched on the edge of the quarry. And he dreamed strange dreams about the Prof, and Jabu, and a strange man with a lock of his hair, staring timelessly into a blazing fire…

CHAPTER 2: PLAYING

"Cows are born with ears; later they grow horns."
Nuba-Tira proverb (Sudan)

He woke to a bright new world. Durban, even in winter, welcomes the sun through the sea-facing windows of the great beach front edifices along Marine Parade. And even now, in July, where it is winter below the Tropic of Capricorn, the sun brings warmth and sparked an optimism in Charlie's heart that he hadn't felt the night before.

He glanced at his watch on the bedside table. It's only 7.30am and Durban is moving. The street cleaners are out, the beach sweepers are busy, the amusement park across the road is being spruced up for the millionth time.

Charlie got up and wandered down for breakfast. The Royal is not just pleasant, it's seriously posh.

The cleaning ladies are all along the corridor busily preparing to repair the rooms... and no, he hasn't yet seen a white person hard at work.

Even in the restaurant, apart from the *maitre de*, the staff are uniformly black and uniformed. And not like your everyday restaurant staff in Portsmouth.

A big man approaches offering coffee. He looks at Charlie's training top. "Ah," he grins, his voice deep, sincere, "Chaka Royals. You are the new Englishman! Good luck my man, you'll need it!"

Charlie grins and holds out a hand. The waiter reels back in shock, then recovers himself and shakes, shyly. "It's not luck I need mate, it's a couple of quick wingers who can put in a decent cross!".

The waiter grins, delighted. "We have got a couple of those... Ace and Junior are quick... and Moses Faya is injured, but when he comes back..."

"So that's it decided then," says Charlie, "Top scorer in a month! What's yer name mate?"

Again, a look of shock on the waiter's face. "Baas," he says, using the Afrikaans term for boss, which carries further connotations of subservience, "My name is Peter, I will be your waiter here, it will be my pleasure."

"And mine," grinned Charlie, "You can fill me in on the local customs Pete!"

Peter, though he looked and sounded like a local Zulu, is a Matabele tribal chief from Bulawayo, a proud man forced into menial labour by new president Robert Mugabe's pro-Shona policies on land.

The previous president, Ian Smith, had been little better to the Matabele, even the faithful ones who served in the old Rhodesian army. But Peter had swallowed his pride and like so many of the white soldiers, he had come south and would send back what money he could afford to feed his wife and four children in the troubled streets of Bulawayo, once a great diamond-trading centre until the mid-60s when the people with the money moved north, worried about Smith's deeply undemocratic Declaration of Unilateral Independence back in 1965.

Charlie finished his breakfast, chatting throughout to Peter, getting a handle on him. He realised that, like the Professor, this was one of those blokes you don't mess with, but immediately trust. Charlie had a feel for these things... though God knows he hadn't met many people he could trust during his formative years.

The men mum had bought home, mostly half-cut, were hardly models of fatherhood. They stayed a few days, stole the rent money from under the pillow, and left. The teachers had judged him before he even walked in the class room, writing him off as a hopeless case because of his drunkard mother and tatty clothes.

Now, suddenly, he was meeting people who, just by the look and sound of them, he felt he could talk to... really open up to.

Charlie shook his head, guessed it was all about the years of being stuck in Fareham, unable to escape the unpleasant legacy his mother seemed intent on leaving him. Nothing. Bills, clutter, a messy council flat next to the rundown pub where she spent her evenings.

And now, here he was, on a tropical beachfront in a five-star hotel, being paid to play football. Incredible.

He walked into the kitchens, looking for Peter, ignoring the stares of the rest of the staff. A white guy walked up: "Can I help you sir?"

"Uh, yeah, I wanted to have a chat with the waiter, Peter. I was hoping he could show me around. I'm here to play football, need a bit of help getting around the city."

The white man, with the word "Koos" on his lapel badge, allowed a slight look of disdain to cross his ruddy face. He wrinkled his moustache at the British accent, bridled at the idea black Peter could do such a job: "Sir it would be a lot better if I got one of the white under-managers to show you around, I..."

"Nah, it's okay... ah, there you are Peter, I was just asking Coos (he pronounced it like the plural of a pigeon call, which further enraged the Afrikaner, Koos, pronounced a little like Coors, the American beer, only without the r) if you could show me around."

Peter looked instantly pleased, then saw the look of displeasure on Koos's face. "Erm, Charlie, I..."

"I'll pay," said Charlie, "Look, here, have ten quid Coos, mate..."

Koos softened instantly. Pounds were growing stronger all the time and this was a valuable green slice of England he was waving around.

"Take an hour Pete, but don't get above yourself," said Koos, and muttered something under his breath which sounded suspiciously like the word "Kaffir" used with such obvious hatred by Merv the night before.

Peter, grinning, threw off his white waiter's coat. It was like the big man had lost ten years... and a stone or two. He positively skipped down the hotel steps, walking out of the front door of the Edward to a frown from the uniformed doorman. "The Bantu entrance is around the back..." he started.

But by now Peter Ndlovu, chief-cum-waiter-cum-guide and Charlie were walking off towards the beach in deep conversation about the troubled transition of Zimbabwe.

Pete was surprised to find an Englishman, especially one with such a strong accent, with such a knowledge of his continent. Of the particular problems in what had once been Rhodesia. Charlie barely knew which knife and fork to use at breakfast, had no idea how to approach people in a larnie hotel but still, he was a bright boy, eager to gather opinions.

Their conversation, earnest and forthright, soon attracted the attention of the two grey-uniformed coppers walking the front. Amidst the growing crowd of tourists – mostly huge Afrikaners from 400 miles inland – the sight of the big black man and the athletic white man chatting so freely was, well... awkward, unusual. The copper cut in as they walked up to the pair: "This man bothering you sir?"

Charlie frowned. To his untutored ears, the question had come out as "Thus mun bovverung you sur?" Peter instantly changed from intelligent conversation to the expected subservience of the South African black man.

"No, sorry baas," he said, "We were just talking, I am showing this Englishman around Durban, he is new to the town..."

"Shut up boy," said the cop, turning to Charlie, "You a rooinek then?"

Charlie hadn't been called a red-neck before, not even in Dutch, where the term recalled the old red coats of the boer war with their sun-burned necks. Charlie laughed: "If that's what you want to call me fine, constable. Is there a problem?"

The policeman, barely 18 and probably a national serviceman straight out of school, liked the Englishman's manner. Easy-going, relaxed, not taking offence. Rare on his beat.

"Ag, no man. Just watch what these blerrie blecks say to you man, never trust a coon!"

Charlie looked at Pete. Pete looked at Charlie. Charlie winked. "Listen to a black man? Never!" said Charlie, laughing overloud, "Be like listening to a chimpanzee!"

They liked that, the two policemen, who began to wander off. Charlie shrugged at Pete. "How do you put up with it," he said, "They were only two thick kids. Give them a uniform and a gun and they think they're God and his best mate."

Pete grinned. "For now, perhaps. No point in making trouble here. Any more talking with the chimp, baas?"

They laughed, wandered through the fair. Pete was unwelcome in the amusement park. Only cleaners and maintenance men of his ilk were acceptable. "So if you go on the dodgems, you reckon they'd arrest you?" asked Charlie, shocked.

"Oh yes, Charlie, no dodgems for blecks! And look at that bench... see what it says "Blankes Alleen"... whites only."

He was right. The toilets. The picnic tables. All carefully labeled, restricted, segregated. "Okay, so what about them," asked Charlie, pointing to a large Asian family who began to sit on and around the picnic table on the strip of green grass next to the fair.

"Watch," said Peter, and the two policemen they'd met earlier began to advance on the family, who quickly got to their feet and left.

"Durban beachfront is whites only, Charlie. Except if there's work to be done early in the morning or late at night. And then, you have to be dressed for the part. Overalls, caps, old takkies (plimsolls or trainers)... and always keep looking at the floor. Never look Baas in the eye."

"This is bollocks, Pete. Nobody talks about this when they discuss South Africa."

"But it happens in England too, Charlie. And in the States, you just look, it's worse there than it was in Zimbabwe under the white government. At least in Bulawayo we could catch a bus with a white man, sit in the cinema, go to the same school if we had the money."

Then, as they approached the beach, a ball came looping off the sands. Several teenagers were having a kick-about. Charlie controlled the ball with a single touch, held it neatly in his instep, then flicked it up, and bowed down to cushion the ball on his neck.

The teenagers laughed and clapped. Charlie let the ball run down his spine, then back-heeled it over his head, where Peter juggled the ball once, twice, three times... and looked like he could keep it there all day.

The teenagers laughed. "Come on, come play," they yelled, "Us three versus you two."

Though neither had anything like the appropriate gear, Peter and Charlie quickly kicked off their shoes, and took up the challenge bare-footed in the firm sand near the crashing waves of the Indian Ocean.

With jumpers for goalposts, the pair of them were in their element; Peter transported back 20 years to his youth and a tennis ball on a street corner, Charlie attempting to show his talent without putting in a tackle of any real significance on the three youngsters.

But it didn't last long. The same two cops came running across the sand, with a small crocodile of concerned, florid sunbathers. "They're playing football on a white beach with our sons," they were lamenting loudly, "It's a scandal. What does this man think he's doing?"

Charlie turned, the coppers were already trying to grab Pete in some sort of armlock. Without appearing to resist arrest, Peter was making it mightily difficult for the two barely-pubescent constables.

Charlie looked at the four or five mums and dads in front of him, so like the parents you'd see at Southsea or Stubbington, but so different inside.

"What harm were we doing?" he asked, "Just playing football, having fun. And you call the police?"

"Ag, you're British," said one of the mothers in a strong Seffeffriken accent, "You don't understand. You let kaffirs play on the beach and the next thing you know they'll be all over the place."

The others nodded in agreement as Peter was frog-marched off the sand. Charlie ran after them: "Hold on guys, this is my fault, you can't just take him, I started kicking the ball and..."

No words, no backward glances. Peter was thrust into the back of the police van... and away.

Charlie was distraught. He ran back to the hotel to tell them. He needed somebody sane, rational. Instead, he got Coos, just walking out of the front door. Koos listened, shrugged. "Stupid vokking kaffir, shouldn't go on a white beach, he'll be back later, moenie worry."

At that precise moment, Jabu pulled up in his big black Valiant, an elegant if slightly-aged American motor. Koos looked at Charlie and muttered something about the friends he was keeping. Charlie tried to fill Jabu in on the disaster which had befallen him and his new friend.

Jabu just smiled. "Charlie, don't worry. Another day in paradise. He'll be out in an hour when they've given him a good telling off. Now I've come to take you for some pictures with the Mercury."

The Natal Mercury was the local morning paper. Though distracted, Charlie attempted to give the local football writer, an elderly white bloke alliteratively called Frank Fraser, a couple of decent quotes.

But to be honest, Frank was more interested in telling Charlie how much he knew about English football, his rounds of golf with Johnny Haynes, the old England captain who had turned up to play for Durban City and how good South African football had been before "they ruined it" and allowed the blacks in.

And when Charlie asked if he was going to his first Royals game on Sunday, Fred shrugged and said: "God, no. It stinks. And they'll have my wallet again. I'll do the local amateur stuff."

Jabu smiled. "It's incredible," he said, "The papers here give more space to the amateur white clubs in the city than they do to the professional clubs. The white clubs get about 100 people to watch, we get 20,000 a game. But they just don't want to cover us. They say they don't think we sell papers but I think it's because the white journalists can't face travelling to the townships to watch us."

They returned to the hotel. Koos was at the front desk. Charlie asked naively: "Coos, can we have a table for two. Lunch?" Koos cackled cruelly. "Ag jou doner Engelsman," he sneered, "What with the fat black guy? In the Royal? I don't think so!"

Then, over his shoulder, Charlie saw Pete. Limping. Awkward. He walked into the restaurant from the kitchens, trying to serve a pair of old ladies in the corner. His arm was clearly hurting as he tried to put the plates in front of them. And his right eye was swollen. Grotesquely.

Charlie could barely take it in. Police brutality over a kickabout on the beach? If they'd done this to a convicted rapist down at the local nick in Fareham there would have been a hell of stink. But not here. Not in good old Durban, where the sun always shines, the bananas grow, the world turns a blind eye to colonialism gone mad.

Charlie was about to react, when Jabu said quietly: "Let it go, don't make a big deal of it Charlie, it's how it is. You kick up and he's the one who'll get more shit. Not you. Leave it."

Charlie gave what he hoped was a look of regret and apology to Pete, who smiled painfully. Jabu shuffled off. "I'll see you at training later, you're here to play football. Remember that. That's what I pay you for, that's what you'll do."

Merv picked him up from the Royal at 5pm. They drove out through the east side of town, past the packed bus queues and along the banks of the Umgeni River, out through the posh white suburbs and then beyond to the motorway and, eventually, the township. The police didn't stop them at the roadblock, they recognised Merv.

The night was drawing in. Not like in the winter in England, but dark and cold nevertheless. Inland it could hit freezing point. Here the Indian Ocean and the warm Mozambique current would keep the temperatures up. Again, Charlie was struck by the rows of hopeless houses, the pall of smoke, the squalor and filth. But amid the chaos, there was a cheerfulness lacking on the plush beachfront. Shouting, laughing, living.

Training in the stadium wasn't too bad. The tension between Vusi and Merv eased when Charlie told the story of his beach football game with Pete... and even Merv agreed: "That's just bloody shocking to beat a bloke up like that for nothing. Okay, we don't want blacks on our beaches but even so...."

While they trained, Charlie became aware of a pair of eyes watching him from high in the Princess Magogo stadium. "Who's the bloke sitting on his own?" asked Charlie.

The Prof smiled: "That's our Sangoma Charlie, our magic man, our witchdoctor as you white guys would say. He makes our luck. He's checking up on you. Making sure you're not the Tokolosh, a bad Leprechaun from across the seas!"

"And this guy helps? How? Surely you don't need a witchdoctor to win a football game?"

"Look Charlie, it's part of our culture. I know the white guys make fun of it but if you like, he's our sports psychologist. He helps us focus on the game, gives us identity, makes us feel good about ourselves.

"And don't tell me you whiteys don't have superstitions before a game. Like doing up one boot before the other or wearing your lucky jock strap. That's really what this guy is. Our lucky charm... our magic 12th man."

Training came and went. The Sangoma never took his mad eyes off Charlie.

Assailed by the day's events, the unsettled Englishman turned to drink that night. The bottom of the bottle had always been an inherited weakness. And boy, could he find the bottom of a bottle.

He fell asleep in his room, the mini-bar tab, hopefully, would be picked up by Jabu. Or somebody. Anybody. That was the way his mother lived… He didn't much like being like that, but sometimes it all gets a bit much for a Hampshire lad in a strange land.

By Saturday, Charlie was getting into some kind of rhythm. Out for a late run when the hangover had worn off, then a swim in the sea. Lunch and a surreptitious chat with Peter as he recovered from his wounds.

"It's nothing, Charlie," he said, "A couple of punches, a kick or two. At least they didn't get the electrodes out!"

The big Matabele chief knew how to take it on the chin, but the guilt was difficult to escape. Charlie had caused Peter's pain. But then, so too had the cops. And the system. The strange, ridiculous doctrine of separation which ran this country.

The evening training sessions were Charlie's favourite part of the day. He found he was fitter than most of his team-mates, despite his current late-night drinking binges.

He was harder too. Fareham Town might be a non-League side, several rungs down the ladder even from the lower reaches of England's world renowned third and fourth divisions. But they were hard men down there. Tough, indomitable… able to play in mud, snow, hail or shine.

But these Zulu lads, Ace, Vusi, Teenage, particularly The Prof, were a bit special on the ball. They could weave magic, a sorcery produced from years with a tennis ball on a street corner. Pele, the great Brazilian, claimed to have learned all he knew from playing with a grapefruit in the favelas. In the townships of Africa, it was a tennis ball on the street corner. Balancing the ball on the foot, the shoulder, the back of the neck, even the forehead.

And as his first game approached, Charlie's anticipation grew. With lads like this to create goals for his direct, no-nonsense style in the penalty area, he could really be on to a good thing here. They knew instinctively where he wanted the ball, what pace to put on it, when to play him through.

And his overwhelming gratitude for a good pass, so different from Merv or the other white guys they had known, gave Charlie an increasingly popular profile in the camp. Even Vusi smiled occasionally, a quizzical look in his eye. The Prof had clearly had a word. He'd put Merv down. And rumours of his run-in with the beachfront coppers had spread around the camp. Charlie, they were starting to realise, was not quite like the average British immigrants they got around these parts.

"We've got Umlazi All Stars on Sunday," coach Fox growled after Friday night's training. "They're our local rivals. They're from the other big Durban township, about 20 miles south near the airport.

"The big workers' hostels are right near their place at the Glebelands Stadium. It's a tight ground, takes about 16,000. But they can make a noise, create an atmosphere. And they've got a couple of players."

Fox glared at Charlie. The rest of the team knew all this. "They'll try to kick you off the park. They've got a big Irish centre half, Ben Anderson. He played Gaelic Football. Left Donegal for United. Didn't make it, came over here. He'll have you. And don't expect protection. The ref might not be up to the old FA's standards back home.

"Ride his tackles, take the punishment. Don't lose your temper, Charlie. The ref will do you, the crowd will get on your back. You're good enough to score a hat-full against this lot, if you can keep your head."

Charlie nodded. Winked at The Prof. As they walked away from their final pre-match training session, Charlie said to the lads: "This Anderson bloke might kick me up in the air, but I've got a few tricks of my own," he grinned, "And if he kicks any of you lot, God help him."

It was said with conviction. The team warmed to their Englishman. Always confident, never cowed. Vusi cleared his throat. "Erm, Charlie. This Anderson. He's a bad man. And they've got another centre-half, Cedric Ndibe. He sharpens his studs, wears a ring which will cut you. He has spikes in his socks too. They'll be after you. The word has gone around our people. A few of their spies have been up in the stands here, taking a look at you.

"I wouldn't say this to many white guys, but I don't want you hurt. I want you to know what you're in for."

By the time Sunday dawned, Charlie could barely contain himself. He kept himself to himself over the weekend. Cut down on the rum and coke. Stopped trying to chat up the barmaid for a couple of evenings.

And he was ready for anything. Except "Mad-Eyes" Dlamini.

Merv drove him into the ground, sneering at the vast mob gathering outside the Glebe Stadium.

Despite his role as the Royals' hard man with the long throw in, Merv was guided through the crowds. His car was treated like a royal limousine, the millions of laughing faces opening a path to the gates of the stadium for the two white men.

There were police vans at every vantage point. A vague whiff of tear-gas as they drove up. The great green gate opened. Charlie found himself in a small compound behind the changing rooms, men were running in and out of gates with bags of cash taken from the gathering fans.

Charlie walked through the iron gates at the back of the changing room complex, it was unfussy, concrete. And there was the Sangoma, staring at him.

He whispered something as Charlie shook his hand. A strong hand, a firm grip. He could have sworn he heard Dlamini say: "Your father was from Ghana" but he must have misheard.

Charlie and the others were gathered in front of the dressing room. The tunnel leading out onto the field lay ahead. They were all talking. Charlie walked on, out of the tunnel, past the tiny dugouts, underneath the radio commentators. It was half-time in some kind of curtain raiser between two lower league sides.

He smiled at the sweating lads sitting in neat semi-circles around their white coaches. He walked out on to the park, focused on the game to come, judging the state of the ground, considering which boots to wear. Six studs or molded? He didn't hear the growing buzz of the crowd.

He walked towards one of the goals, examining the worn strip down the middle of the ground, the bare goalmouth, pitted, nasty.

Then the crowd began to roar as he approached the goal itself. They didn't like it, and Charlie was suddenly aware of their antipathy.

"Tokolosh!" they screamed, gold Umlazi scarves and flags waving. He was headed towards the home end and, apparently, they didn't like him walking towards their goal.

A huge man, with a long lens camera hanging from his neck, came running towards him. It was the Mercury photographer he'd met briefly on Monday. "Baas! Englishman! Go back! They think you are bad muti... you cannot go across the goal-line before the match, not here, it will spoil their spells!"

Charlie stopped. Gazing at the bank of angry fans, screaming abuse and exotic curses at him. The opposition's Sangoma was approaching from the corner flag. Charlie walked towards him, surprisingly confident, at ease. He felt like he was born for this moment.

In his best Zulu, he said: "Sabona, umfowetu," and held out his hand. "I see you brother." The rival medicine man was nonplussed. White men didn't say such things, not without malice in their eyes. But there was something in this Englishman's manner.

The Sangoma made a quick decision. He smiled, put a big arm around the Englishman's shoulders, and the crowd roared their approval. Charlie waved at the crowd... and in a moment he would never quite understand, he slipped his wrist watch off his arm and threw it into the crowd, where it created something of a scrum.

The All Stars fans liked that. A lot. The Sangoma smiled. In easy, cultured English, he said: "You will be a fine rival, Englishman. You know the ways of our people. Your father was from Accra."

Charlie walked off to resounding applause from both the gold and green ends of the ground. Jabu and the Mercury photographer, Solomon, were stunned: "You're lucky they didn't jump the fence and murder you for walking towards their goal like that," said Jabu. "How did you know what to do? To give them a gift shows respect. And from a white man, that's important. It's everything. You've just made things a lot easier for yourself. I knew you'd be a good investment!"

Dlamini wasn't so sure. "That induna is not to be trusted, Charles. Come."

And so, into the dressing room. A tall, powerful-looking ref shook his hand. "Welcome Englishman, but behave yourself. I know your sort. You think you know better than us African referees."

Charlie smiled. "No way ref. You do the toughest job of all. You tell me to jump, and I'll ask how high!"

Jabu laughed. Dlamini took it all in. "He's the best ref in the country," said The Prof, "As long as you're a black boy!"

"My dad's from Lagos!" laughed Charlie. Dlamini went into the changing room first. To prepare.

Vusi went out to the edge of the pitch, where the curtain raiser was being played at a frantic pace. He took a small trowel and dug a sod of earth from the touchline. Some of the Umlazi fans noticed and began to shout. Vusi returned, fast. Charlie went out to distract them, waving and handing them hotel front desk sweets, slighty dusty, from his pocket.

Vusi grinned. The players stood behind Vusi at the dressing room doorway. He gently spread the soil from the pitch across the threshold. Dlamini had already deposited soil from the Princess Magogo in KwaMashu.

One by one, the players undid their flies... and urinated in great arcs on the earth-covered concrete of the dressing room. Charlie was tempted to laugh, but everyone looked quite serious. Merv and Andy simply walked through the sludge... but Charlie stopped, whipped out his willy, and had a quick pee in support of his team-mates.

Vusi watched. Dlamini glowered.

Clive started his pre-match team-talk while they walked to their numbered shirts, hung on pegs around the room.

Dlamini stood over a cauldron in the middle of the dressing-room. He was dropping various trinkets and bits of material into the cauldron, which had a small butane gas canister flaring beneath it. A bit of gold wool, a few blades of grass, a key, a piece of string, perhaps from the goal net. A referee's whistle, a page from *Ilanga*, the Zulu newspaper.

The whole concoction was stirred, Fanny Craddock style, into a slimey mix. Dlamini picked up some of the sludge from the doorway and added it, gently, bringing his recipe to the boil. Then he took a ribbon of green material, dipped it into his simmering soup, and tied it carefully around the goalkeeper, Henry's, midriff.

The process was repeated for each member of the squad, even Merv and Andy. Charlie suppressed the need to giggle again. He focused on Fox's detailed team-talk, his breakdown of the opposition's tactics.

While Dlamini tied the ribbon around him, underneath his green No10 shirt, Charlie listened as Fox explained the ponderous but dangerous nature of the Umlazi centre-back pairing. "Lumbering oxen they may be, but if either of them get hold of Charlie..."

Dlamini began to chant. The air around him seemed to vibrate. The Prof started to talk. The Zulu lads closed their eyes. Merv and Andy went quiet, their endless tales of female conquest curtailed for ten minutes.

Charlie closed his eyes. Uncertain of his role in these proceedings. Even Clive Fox was silent. Reality began to slip. Charlie glimpsed a thousand fur-clad warriors charging over a ridge, heard the sound of distant muskets... could have sworn he heard drums, the thud of wildebeest hooves on an open plain.

And then it was over. They were running out, green next to gold, KwaMashu versus Umlazi. Fourth against eighth in the National Soccer League.

Charlie was still in a bit of a muddle for the first ten minutes. The huge referee, George Thebe, laughed as he was cut down mercilessly by the huge ginger-haired Anderson whenever he tried to receive the ball to feet.

He heard the vague shouts from Fox, the odd roar from Jabu. Umlazi scored, the stadium erupted – all but the green end, towards Durban.

A jet flew over, leaving a long vapour trail across the clear blue sky. A small boy was crying by the perimeter fence. There was a mangy dog running between the crowd behind the goal. Not Fareham. Charlie was confused but serene. It wasn't like anything he'd experienced before. But there was magic in the air.

A throw-in near the halfway line. Half-an-hour gone. Merv to take it, long. The Prof whispered in his ear: "Now, Charlie. For God, for Queen, for country!"

Charlie laughed out loud. Instinctively, he began to run on a long curving parabola around the back of the two huge centre-backs.

Merv's throw cut through the air, Charlie could almost see the vapour trail. Anderson, frantic, turned as the ball landed, bounced unevenly, but Charlie, with his back to goal, took it down perfectly.

His touch was sure, his head clear. This was his job. His moment. Anderson came charging in from behind. Referee George had a sly grin on his face. As the ball fell at his feet, Charlie could sense the big Irishman rampaging in from behind. Sonny, the Royals most ineffectual midfielder, was screaming for the ball to feet. Fox shouted: "Man on, play the way you're facing..."

Charlie did nothing of the sort. He simply backheeled the ball through Anderson's legs in a sublime moment which owed something to years of being clattered in Hampshire... and perhaps a little to Dlamini's stinking ribbon of sorcery around his middle.

He leapt in the air, turning. Anderson swept through beneath him like a super tanker midway through its turning circle, sliding helplessly against the tide.

The other huge centre-half roared in on the slide, his sharpened studs reaching for the ball, his trailing boot aiming for Charlie's privates. "Easy Cedric," he cried and flipped the ball over the onrushing defender. He hurdled the challenge, and with both full-backs charging in from either side, he ignored The Prof's warning: "Man on Charlie!" Now he was an artist. Or was it Geoff Hurst! As the ball bounced, with both feet off the floor, Charlie lashed out his "wrong" foot, his left, and both full-backs clattered into him. As he fell, twisting, Charlie saw the ball curve into the top corner of the net, every detail of the watching fans' faces etched in his mind. Even the mongrel amid the crowd looked surprised.

"Gooooooal!" screamed the radio reporters in three Bantu languages in their little hutches atop the concrete block of the dressing rooms. "Gooooooal!" screamed the 3,000 Royals fans at the far end of the ground.

As he wriggled from under the bodies of the vanquished defenders, Charlie rose to be greeted by his team, including the surprisingly rapid goalkeeper, Henry, who had emerged from his penalty area in a show of pure triumph.

On the touchline, Dlamini was performing some sort of foot-stomping war-dance. Jabu was putting his jelly-like belly through a pitch-line celebration and the Fox simply howled. There were no television cameras to catch his first goal in Africa. But Charlie didn't need a video replay to recall every detail of his wonder-strike years later in various bars from Petersfield to Pretoria.

A furious Ben Anderson spat on Charlie's back as he ran past, arms aloft. But Charlie barely noticed. This was why he had travelled 5,000 miles, this was what he'd always wanted. A full-house, a vital goal, the acclamation of the fans.

And it wasn't over yet.

Half-time passed him by. The fans, whether for lack of facilities or superstition, gathered at the perimeter fence to urinate onto the pitch. Vendors were cooking strange meat dishes on open fires in the stands. Charlie was distracted. Fox said a lot but it was mostly waffle. Charlie had learnt to listen to The Prof's quiet asides. "Give it to Ace, get Charlie down the middle. Get the cross in. Charlie will beat them in the air."

Charlie had played against great centre-backs on their way down. He'd played young defenders on their way up. And many in between. They'd all kicked him, but by and large he respected them.

It was the cloggers he couldn't stand. The ones who had no talent other than an ability to kick and swear, rant and spit. Ben and Cedric were, unquestionably and without apology, such lumping louts. And Charlie relished the chance to expose their lack of real talent.

It took twenty minutes. Ace broke fast down the left, weaving his magic in and out of the midfielder, then the despairing full-back. The cross, when it came, was far from perfect, bobbling perhaps on the goat's head buried somewhere in the pitch overnight by Dlamini, or so The Prof had said.

It came like a rifle shot, knee high, Anderson prepared to put an uncultured boot to it, the keeper yelled: "Get it out! Anywhere will do."

Charlie threw himself headlong towards the ball, toward's the Irishman's merciless toe-cap before the two objects converged. Charlie's diving header was perfectly timed. He angled the ball into the near corner of the net, and took the boot firmly on the back of his head. The pain was nothing. The glory of his second goal was everything.

Anderson couldn't believe it. Neither could Umlazi's Scottish coach, Billy McGivern, screaming, shouting. "That's fooking ridiculous," he yelled, "I told you to kill the English bastard!"

Anderson's assassination attempted had failed. Blood streaming from his now-wounded head, Charlie refused to take the acclaim of fans behind the goal alone, running instead to Ace and holding his light frame high. Then he broke the clinch and yelled "You're the man, Ace!" The fans loved it. He could have sworn he saw George, the referee, break into a creaking smile. Then Charlie fell over, dizzy but happy, his head wound throbbing.

Problem was, as medicine man, Dlamini was the official physio for the Royals. Whatever he'd been trained in, it wasn't classic boy scout first aid. He wrapped all kinds of bandages around Charlie's head, some foul-smelling goo, pulled out something that might have been a rabbit's foot and said: "Go, Englishman. Scare the Irishman."

As it happened, he didn't need to. Anderson chopped him down on the edge of the area with ten minutes left. The ref had gone soft and gave a free-kick. The Prof, incredibly, produced one of his left-leg-around-the-back-of-right-leg scissor kicks from the dead-ball and the Umlazi keeper's first sighting of the ball was when it had nestled neatly in the back of the net.

And that was it. A crushing 3-1 win, two for "Cheerful Charlie" as the old-fashioned Mercury described him the next day. And his career was firmly underway on African soil.

Jabu was a happy man. Not just with the sensational goals Charlie had conjured... but with the response he was getting to his cheap-but-cheerful Englishman from all quarters.

Often white players were booed by their home fans, who preferred to see eleven home boys in action. KwaZulu fans were quite sophisticated, they understood the need for reinforcements from abroad, whatever their colour.

But they rarely warmed to them. The exiled Germans, the

mercenary Chileans, the knock-kneed Malawian, a pretend Italian...even, remarkably, a real Russian. All had scored for the Royals over the years.

But none had been received with the warmth being offered to Charlie after the game. Dlamini, no great lover of the white man, was positively glowing. Horatio Motlane, the township leader and unofficial mayor, forced his way into the dressing room to shake the boy's hand. Even George, the ref, had good words to say.

And as they drove away from Glebelands, Jabu witnessed the really astonishing sight of Umlazi fans clapping KwaMashu's new English hero.

He was a bit special, this Charlie. Jabu was a happy man.

CHAPTER 3: SETTLING:

"When a tree falls on a yam farm and kills the farm's owner, you don't waste time counting the numbers of yam hips ruined."
                                        Igala proverb (Nigeria)

THE next morning, his head throbbing, Charlie awoke in his hotel room. They had retired to a shebeen after the game. Jabu, the proprietor, had encouraged his Englishman to sample the local sorghum beer. Bits of something bitter floated in the thick liquid, but blimey, it had a kick.

Charlie had been surprised to see good-looking, western-dressed Zulu girls in the pub. Make-up, short skirts and shiny s-curls. And they spoke passable English, unlike Charlie after three beers. Teenage, his co-striker who looked 17 from a distance but was probably in his early thirties, encouraged them to flirt with this strange foreigner, who appeared to be colour blind in all ways.

Charlie had loved it. At least the parts he could remember. Vusi and his non-footballing buddies had shunned him at first. Until, boldened by "Kaffir beer" and his heroic status, Charlie had muscled in among them and given his team-mate a massive hug. "You were superb today Vusi," he roared, "You should be playing for Arsenal."

Embarrassed, Vusi had mumbled a few words, but with his friends breaking in to broad smiles, he began to chat and the evening had ended with intense political debate. Vusi's mates were well-read Marxists, socialists... "labour voters" he laughed, "Viva the revolution!" He lifted the universal symbol of a clenched fist... and then he fell asleep at the table. Head down. Bang.

He thought he'd been okay, not over-chummy, but clearly one of the lads. Merv and Andy hadn't even stayed. They'd gone off to celebrate in town, whoring down Point Road no doubt.

Charlie had no idea how he'd got home to the hotel. Luck rather than judgment. And he knew Jabu and The Prof were always looking out for him. A Mercury had been pushed under the door. He scoured the back pages. Hmm. The actual back page consisted of a semi-political "Idler" column, supposedly a laugh-a-minute social commentary. Sport inside, it said.

Inside, they'd spread on Saturday's rugby. Natal were only a B section side in the Currie Cup, watched by around 11,000 at the vast bowl of King's Park in the centre of town. They'd lost to Griqualand West, a tiny province, capital Kimberley, home of the Big Hole, a massive open diamond mine. Years later, the local rugby side would amount to something. But not in the early 1980s.

The real sporting focus of the weekend, the local derby between Umlazi and KwaMashu, was relegated to a strip beneath a page devoted to the amateur "white" league. Every match in the Natal Premier League received its own report and pictures. Ridiculous.

But hey, there it was. "Cheerful Charlie is a Royal success" said the headline, written by one of their sports sub-editors after a quick phone call to Clive Fox. Fogey Fred hadn't bothered to go to the big local derby, the best-attended sporting event of the week around Durban.

But Charlie's spectacular goals were featured in the piece, as was the fact that Jabu's men were now third behind the Sowetan giants, Kaizer Chiefs and Orlando Pirates. And there was a picture. A fine one taken by the big photographer, Solomon, who had helped him when he wandered on the pitch.

It showed Charlie lifting Ace Ntsoeleng high in the air, with blood pouring down the back of his shirt. The caption: "Bloody hero: English import celebrates his second goal, a fine dive-header, with one of the Royals players". They couldn't even tell one Royal from another. And it didn't appear to bother the Mercury one jot.

But if Charlie thought the poor coverage of his first big match would lend him anonymity, he was wrong.

The television, radio and newspapers in this strange land were dominated by "white" sport. Plenty of rugby and cricket, a little bit of athletics, even polo up the north coast, bowls for the white pensioners. Oh, and strange Afrikaans games like Jukskei – a variation on hoop throwing - and Korfbal, a form of netball for men.

But 16,000 people had been at Glebelands watching football, the universal game. Thousands more had listened to their radios. And then there was the oral tradition of the Zulu, spreading news of the township's new hero up and down the coastline faster than a midwinter bush fire.

When he went for breakfast, Peter was first to congratulate him. "Englishman, you are a hero!" he smiled, "I tried to get to the game, but the police stopped our taxi. I hear your first goal was a wondrous thing to behold!"

Charlie grinned. "Their two centre-backs were like Laurel and Hardy, Peter. In a war they'd be cannon-fodder mate. Big, thick men who can knock down little boys but if they meet somebody with a bit of talent, they're a pushover. Nothing more, nothing less. Not true warriors like you and me!"

Peter loved that. He would tell of his conversation with the Royal Englishman all week. And he would cherish the tickets Charlie would push in his hands for the next game.

The chefs in the kitchens wanted to cook him something special. The chambermaids giggled as he approached. The doorman would have polished his shoes with his tongue. For a lad largely ignored by his own mother, bullied for his swarthiness and ragged clothes at school and largely overlooked as a youth at Portsmouth, this was one of the great days.

He wandered with Peter along Marine Parade. It felt like everyone wanted to talk to them. The same two policemen walked past, glaring at the little gaggle of blacks around the pair. Charlie caught their eye. Walked over. "We're doing no harm," he said, "If you ever bothered to speak to the people you police, you might just learn to like them. And they might start to like you."

"Ag Engelsman," said the blonde one, "You understand nothing about South Africa. We wiped the floor with the Zulu at the Battle of Blood River. This is our land, they want it back. It will always be a war. God helps us to win the war every single day."

Charlie had done some reading. He knew enough to respond: "You had guns and wagons at Blood River. They had spears and shields and a couple of rusty muskets. It wasn't God, it was bloody technology."

The two policemen surged forward, fists clenched. Charlie backed off but continued the argument. "You continue to treat them like the enemy, like second class citizens in their own country, and you'll be in real trouble in a few years. Remember how you guys felt when the British ran this country and they made you stand in the corner with a dunce cap on if you spoke Afrikaans? That was wrong too. I apologise for it. And the Boer War concentration camps."

That held them. Johannes and Balthazar. Two raw Afrikaans policemen, both barely 17. They didn't know what to make of this one. The conversation might have gone on, probably ending in an arrest and a few uncomfortable nights, had Peter not quietly whisked Charlie off.

Charlie was given the night off training. He'd thought stitches would be required in his head wound, but Dlamini's peculiar first aid seemed to have sealed the wound quite effectively. He had bruises over most of the rest of his body though.

But without football he was bored. Peter wouldn't come out with him, he didn't fancy a night with Andy and Merv, who had also been given the night off. So he went down to Coconuts, a bar and cabaret joint in the Main Hotel, a lively establishment further down the beachfront.

Alone, he ate in the restaurant and listened to a couple of stale British comedians trying to get a chuckle out of the holidaying South Africans. Under Apartheid, there were few foreigners on vacation along this magnificent sea front. Just inlanders, mostly Afrikaans. But Charlie struck up a couple of conversations, managed to find enough people who knew a little about Fulham and Arsenal, Chelsea and Manchester United.

He was happily chatting to a bunch of ex-pats when a gaggle of women bubbled into the bar. Big, blousy women. They were speaking English, not Afrikaans. The men he was with greeted them in an off-hand sort of way. And Charlie realized these were the wives, who'd been out on some sort of ladies' night in another bar. This was the point of a slightly awkward reunion.

The men didn't mention the illicit stripper who'd been on earlier in the afternoon, the women wouldn't let them overhear how one of their number had whipped her top off when a lithe group of lifeguards had entered their bar earlier in the night.

Charlie chatted on with the men, mostly printers and engineers from Mobeni, the industrial area down the South Coast road towards Umlazi. Most had been in Durban a decade, all still referred to Britain as "home", listened to the BBC World Service for the football scores on a Saturday and considered Benny Hill the ultimate in comedy.

From the sound of it, they all lived in luxury compared to their old pre-emigration lives. From terraced houses and postage-stamp gardens, they had graduated fairly quickly in South Africa to sprawling homes with half-acre gardens and swimming pools.

Of course they complained about the large local insects, the lack of traditional British goods in the shops, the terrible local television (the anti-Apartheid Equity performers' union prevented quality English programming from travelling 5,000 miles south)… and of course, they had little time for the indigenous populace, or the Asians. Universally maligned for being untrustworthy and dangerous, most of them ended any discussion of the disenfranchised with the classic line: "Africa's great, pity about the Africans."

Perhaps that's why Charlie lost concentration with the beer-swilling men around him. He'd tried to put the alternative view rather than the alter-native view. He'd patiently begun explaining this was Zulu country and British immigrants were the visitors rather than the other way round. But nobody listened. He was a new arrival. Didn't know what he was talking about.

His eyes roved slowly around the bar. He'd been reasonably popular with the girls in Fareham. His footballing exploits were a minor talking point and though he had little idea of fashion, he wasn't in bad shape compared to some of his tubby mates.

And the same applied tonight. Amid the tipsy, beer-bellied hubbies, Charlie stood out like a beacon.

And one of the wives had noticed. Across the dance floor, amid the gaggle of mostly overweight, fading women from the home counties and beyond, was Caroline.

Boredom had been her greatest enemy since she and George had arrived in Durban nine years before. She had worked in a factory in Dagenham, doing the kind of conveyor belt job only blacks did in South Africa.

She hadn't really been qualified for anything else, other than giving birth and looking good on her husband's arm. He had been a dockyard worker in Britain. Here he ran a yard of strong, hardworking Zulus, and he had risen rapidly up the ladder on the back of their labour. George liked to tell his jealous mates back home in Essex how hard he was on his gang, how he had to show them he was "the baas".

In truth, it was hard to fail in his position down the docks. White and articulate, heartless in his approach to the workforce, George had provided well for the beautiful Caroline and the three slightly-spoiled kids now attending the best schools in Durban.

Caroline couldn't argue with that. But she was bored. She ran every morning, played tennis with the other rich housewives around Kloof on the inner-edge of the City, and generally did good, charitable works.

But occasionally the old Essex girl in her would creep out. It had happened several times, generally in the kind of situation she found herself in now.

She knew she was beautiful. Stunning in comparison to the other British wives around her.

She'd had a few Cinzanos and Charlie was in her sights. She was the Great White Huntress, with perfect breasts and a cheater's rapid thighs.

Charlie had noticed as much. The Police came on the sound system, some of the wives got up to dance. Charlie noticed a couple of the young singles from the other side of the bar rise too, the dance floor became something of a groped-off area as bored housewives and young students paired up.

The husbands barely noticed. Charlie got up, the current topic under discussion was the how to get *The Sun* into the country with the topless girl on page three not ruined by the censor's black pen.

Caroline was gyrating on her own, rebuffing any hopeful youngster aiming for first prize on his big night out.

Her eyes met Charlie's as he moved onto the floor. He was the chosen one. Clearly. One problem. He couldn't dance. He could barely move from one foot to the other and click his fingers in time. Something to do with not having sisters. Given that everyone seemed to think his father was descended from some long-lost African, he was kind of hoping a genetic sense of rhythm would rise in him now.

No such luck. He did his normal awkward gyrating in the corner, hoping Caroline wasn't looking.

She was. And she was good-looking too. Stunning. Blonde. Pink glittery dress, tight in all the right places, accentuating good hips, a trim waist, flat stomach, full breasts and, something Charlie always noticed, good upper arms.

So many women had purple, flaccid arms, it was a sign of what was just around the corner. Not Caroline. She had been born beautiful, and the daily exercise forced on her by boredom had kept her so. She was, at 5ft 10in, about two inches shorter than Charlie but taller than every other woman in the room. Her blue eyes and high cheek bones dominated the dance floor. Her ridiculously high heels failed to hamper her sleek movement towards him. Bee-line, sting at the ready.

Charlie felt like he was about to receive a suicide pass, a Hail Mary. As he took the ball, he would be scythed down from behind. And besides, he had Sarah at home. Though he doubted she was being particularly faithful at this point.

But as so often in these situations, he reacted with unexpected aplomb for one so naturally awkward.

"High gorgeous, you're Caroline from Dagenham," he grinned, "George and his mates have told me all about you."

His opening line failed to take the wind from her sails. He might as well have tried the less defensive: "Fancy a shag?"

Her hand gripped his arm, her long red finger nails, complete with wedding band, dug into his brown skin.

"Don't mess me about darling, take me outside. Now."

Charlie was used to forward Fareham floozies. But this was something else. Her husband, the father of her three children, was barely 20 yards away. Charlie was intensely aware of his presence and drew back, trying to think of slightly chubby Sarah with the mousy hair back in Fareham.

Think. Focus. This was a non-runner. Caroline was gorgeous but alarm bells were clanging loudly in his head, his heart… and other parts. Yet all around him, the wives were desperately trying to recapture their teenage years with a quick grope and a snog from the student types in the disco. And the hubbies were oblivious.

"You're not one of those gay homosexuals are you?" she asked, her perfect mouth and exotic eye-lashes offering a physical sophistication to her base Estuarine accent.

"Erm, no, I'm not gay," said Charlie, reddening, "Just slightly worried about my girl-friend back home, not to mention the unhappily-married husband's union over there."

"Don't worry," said Caroline, "He hasn't shagged me for years. Comes to bed drunk every night, stinking of perfume. He's not a man, he's a fat golfer who brings in the bacon, fucks his sad secretary and talks about football."

"Yeah well, that'll be me after a few years of marriage!" said Charlie, making light of the over-harsh assessment of a husband who clearly provided well for his wife and children.

Charlie was a bit old-fashioned when it came to marriage. Given his mother's plight, Charlie felt marriage was a proper institution, something not to be taken lightly. He might have had the odd fling – what was it, four women since his first knee-trembler outside the legion at 17 – but he was saving himself for the right woman.

Caroline looked like that girl. But didn't act like it. And she must have been ten years older than him.

"I want you," she said, gripping his arm harder and brushing her luscious body against his, "You can't let me go home like this. I'll have to resort to the vibrator again... and George hates that. The buzzing keeps him awake."

She was calculated. Her words unsettled and titillated in equal measure. He'd had a bit to drink, she was sensationally good looking, the pick of the bunch. One snog would put him top of the table in this dingy disco. All the students were looking, the wives were staring. They were the chosen couple... would they take the risk?

Charlie looked deep into her eyes. He looked for a sign of his mother in Caroline's gaze. Weakness, fecklessness. Yes, she'd had a drink, but this was no hopeless offering of an obese, unwanted body. This was a beautiful woman offering a night of pleasure the like of which he could barely imagine. Fantasy time.

She glared back, unflinching. She was used to winning in these situations. Nobody resisted her charms. She only lost battles at home. With George. Over spending, normally on clothes... or an addition to her 82 pairs of shoes.

Every stray, good-looking man was putty in her hands. And she knew it. She shoved her chest out, allowing her breasts to brush his arm. She pushed herself against him, swaying to the music, a siren, a temptress.

Charlie moved with her, allowing her to excite him, make him hard. He tightened his thighs, his chest, his biceps. She was drinking him in with those deep blue eyes.

Breathless, she murmured: "Let's get out of here, take me to a hotel. Leave quickly, wait a hundred yards down on the right. You'd better be good, I need it all night."

Charlie was out of his depth now. He turned abruptly and walked. The wives, quite happy to share this affair vicariously, were almost salivating. One of them grabbed a handful of his tight buttock as he passed. The women whooped. Caroline smiled wickedly.

Charlie hit the door, the cold air hit him… and he knew he couldn't do it. He couldn't do it to the husband. To the kids. To himself. Or Caroline. Or Sarah.

He walked quickly away from the beat of the music, he reached the hotel in ten minutes, stormed upstairs and spent the best part of an hour under a cold shower, trying to sober up, work out if he'd just missed out on the greatest night of his life… or avoided one of the worst mistakes in his insubstantial love life. Now he'd never know.

Caroline occupied his thoughts for most of his morning run, he was nearly bloody tumescent by the time he plunged into the surf to cool down.

At lunch he found himself looking closely at any passing blonds, comparing them unfavourably to the sizzling siren of the night before.

Jabu came to pick him up for training. "Merv's not coming," he explained, "He wants a pay rise after making your first goal on Sunday. Thinks he's worth more than he's paid."

"Is he?" asked Charlie. Jabu snapped: "Of course not. Andy and Merv are on twice as much as anyone else in the side. More than you too. The white guys always want too much. Half the side would play for free, for the glory of representing the Royals. But Merv, he shows no respect, he's rude, he fights, he drinks, he smokes dope…"

"Great long throw though boss!" said Charlie, and both men were laughing as a car appeared alongside them on the motorway, hedging them into the slow lane.

Jabu accelerated, but it was a powerful vehicle next to them, it easily stayed with them, hooting. Charlie was starting to get sweaty. Two big white guys, both with moustaches, filled the front seats. As Charlie looked at the passenger, he pulled a gun from inside his jacket. He smiled, looked at Charlie.... And produced a number plate with three letters emblazoned across it: SAP.

"Oh shit, police," said Jabu. "I thought it was just two madmen trying to kill us," Charlie replied. "Might be the same thing," said Jabu, and pulled over.

The coppers climbed slowly out of the car. "Uit, out, al twee van julle, both of you!"

"Say nothing," Jabu murmured, "They'll be hoping for a cheeky white boy they can push about a bit."

Charlie climbed meekly from the car. The first copper, his gun still drawn, gestured for him to face the vehicle. "Put your hands on the roof. Legs apart." Charlie did as he was told. The policeman moved up behind him, stinking of a truly awful aftershave and cigars. He pushed himself up against Charlie from behind, changing the whole atmosphere. He whispered in Charlie's ear: "You one of those moffies eh? One of those queers who love black cock?"

Charlie didn't react. He kept calm. Visions of Caroline. "No officer, I'm a professional footballer from England. I'm sorry to have troubled you today. Jabu is the chairman of my football club, the Chaka Royals. I am not armed or dangerous."

The policeman sneered: "Soccer hey? With the blecks? Fucking trouble maker. You shouldn't share a car with coons, Englishman. I know your sort."

He searched Charlie roughly, running his hands nastily, suggestively, all over his body. Charlie felt nauseous. The huge, calloused hands moved beween his legs, made quick, heavy contact with his balls. Charlie didn't jump, didn't flinch. The other copper yelled: "Enough Willem, let the Englishman go now. Easy."

Konstabel Willem Coetzee drew back, sweating. Aroused. As he turned, he let his heavy policeman's shoe catch the back of Charlie's heel with some force. Charlie rode the kick, one of the tricks of his trade. He'd seen it coming. The guy wouldn't make a great clogger on the football field.

The other copper patted Jabu's chubby cheek, then pinched it. The last pat was more of a slap. "Jabu," he said, voice filled with contempt, "We know you, we watch you. One step out of line and you'll be off to the resettlement camps in the north my friend. And we'll run your shebeens for you."

Jabu said nothing. Charlie, surprised by his own bravery, said: "We meant no harm officer, I'm just going to training. You can come and watch if you want. The Royals are a good team, you should be proud of them. We could win the League this season."

The other copper, a Sergeant from his insignia, laughed: "You're full of kak, Englishman. You should play rugby, a man's game. Only queers and communists play football. God made us hands to play football with."

Charlie laughed at the contradiction. Then hit back with: "You want a wing for your rugby team, come see me at the Edward Hotel. Seriously."

The sergeant eased, visibly. "You serious?" he said, giving Charlie the once-over. "It's a hard game in this country. We don't take an English winger lightly in South Africa!"

"Neither do the coons when I play football in townships, officer," said Charlie, "They kicked me to shit on Sunday and I still scored twice and left Umlazi alive!"

They both laughed then. Coetzee had calmed down. The thrill of the moment, his power-crazed lust had left him. The old Calvinist in him restored.

"Luister, listen, both of you, just stay out of trouble. There's a big operation going down in KwaMashu tonight, best you don't go into that fucking slum."

With that they were gone. Tweedle-dee and tweedle-dum in matching uniforms. Repressed, angry men… cleverly placated. And Jabu knew it. "Good chat, Charlie," he said, "There's more to you than meets the eye. You'd really play rugby?"

"No way Jabu, it's a game for the barbaric upper classes pal! I do my talking with my feet! Did you see that copper feeling me up?"

"Lots of them are into male rape," said Jabu, "The more racist the Afrikaner, the more likely you are to find him breaking his Dutch Reformed Church commandments. It's strange. They're so good on a Sunday in the kerk, but out in the street, they do anything.

"You'd be amazed how many of the most right-wing politicians are found in the homeland casinos watching pornography and paying for black prostitutes."

"It's a power thing, Jabu. Like the Roman Catholic priests back home. Always got an eye out for a pretty choir boy. One day they'll be exposed. Or go to hell. Or both."

They drove silently towards the Princess Magogo. "What do you think they meant about "a big operation" in KwaMashu, Jabu?" asked Charlie, "Sounds bad. Has there been trouble?"

"Just kids throwing stones at the police cars Charlie. It's what makes us men, young warriors showing their courage."

With that, they turned a corner straight into a police road block. Jabu took in the scene before them. Literally hundreds of grey-uniformed police and dozens of soldiers. All heavily armed, ready for action. You could see it from a mile away. This was serious shit.

Charlie turned to talk to Jabu as three or four cops came walking, with intent, towards the car. The big man had disappeared. Jabu's seat was empty, the car door open. Charlie didn't panic. He got out of the car as the police approached.

"What the fuck are you doing here," asked one of the coppers from the beachfront angrily, "Haven't you had enough shit?"

"Sorry officer," said Charlie, keeping his cool, trying to assess the situation. "Look, I'm a professional footballer. I've only been here a bloody week. I'm on my way to training at the stadium."

The copper glared. "Best you fuck off back to your larnie hotel Englishman. There's going to be big trouble here and you want to be a long, long way away."

Charlie frowned. He wanted to see what was going on, though his instincts were saying flee. "I can't, you scared away my driver," he said, "Honestly, I'm not a trouble maker, just a bloke trying to play football, make a bloody living."

A call came from the gathering of police and army behind them. The coppers lost interest in Charlie, turned and made their way back to the growing ranks of grey and brown.

Charlie sidled up. There were several plain-clothes types around in shirt sleeves. Charlie tried to blend in. He begged a cigarette from one of the officers, and disguised himself with a smoking fag and an intense expression.

In front of him, hidden around the corner from the pot-holed main drag through KwaMashu, the soldiers were piling boxes on the back of a large flatbed truck.

A group of heavily armed men carrying automatic rifles climbed through a hole in the den of cardboard, disappearing from sight on the back of the truck.

Lots of shouting and talking. Then another truck was loaded up in identical fashion. Somebody said "Trojan Horse" in the middle of a long burst of Afrikaans.

After what seemed like an age and three cigarettes, the two trucks pulled slowly onto the main street. Two bakkies, ordinary unmarked pick-up trucks, pulled out behind them, filled with armed police. Charlie jumped on the second one, ignored in the excitement of Operation Trojan Horse.

They turned the corner. Two hundred yards ahead, the two trucks were driving slowly through the usual gathering of heavily-burdened women and street urchins.

From a street to the right, a gang of about 12 young teenagers emerged with red bandannas across their faces. They threw bricks and stones at the trucks, accurate and fast, clearly ready to withdraw into the backstreets in the event of trouble.

Charlie suddenly realised what was about to happen. But before he could yell a warning, Operation Trojan Horse moved swiftly into action.

The boxes were swept aside by the soldiers hidden inside. The truck stopped. Charlie counted eight men armed with automatic rifles. They stood and fired into the street throng. Charlie could hear the dull pop of the guns, watched the bullets rip into women and children. Enraged, the gang of youths picked up anything they could lay their hands on, retreat forgotten as they hurled stones and bottles at the armed men on the back of the truck.

Inevitably the gunmen turned on them, hundreds of rounds tearing into the teenagers and the shacks behind them.

Then the trucks roared off. The coppers on the bakkie around him opened fire with pistols as they drove after the galloping, deadly Trojan Horses.

Charlie leapt off the back of the bakkie, tears flowing, rage in his heart. Three or four black men grabbed him and started punching and kicking him. A chant went up. They had a white policeman. He had fallen off the truck.

Charlie yelled and screamed: "Let me help, get an ambulance, I can…"

But then something broke over the back of his head, and his world went black. Jabu arrived as he fell, pulling the mob away from his centre-forward angrily, supported by Vusi, who was also caught up in the crowd.

They got to Charlie, waving their hands, shouting. Mercifully, he wasn't badly hurt, the kicking hadn't really started. They picked him up, dusted him off.

Consciousness returned. Charlie's vision gradually cleared. "Fucking hell, thanks Jabu, thanks Vusi," he said, "I didn't think. I just couldn't believe what I was seeing…"

Vusi growled: "We've never seen that before either. It's a new tactic. They've used it inland. Bastards."

"Bastards? Murderers, Vusi. Worse than the bloody Nazis. Can you imagine if the British troops tried this in Belfast?"

"We have to get you out of here Charlie, when they realise a white man witnessed this, they'll want to keep you quiet. You'll be a marked man." Jabu said, "There's nothing you can do here, training's off, the season may be off. KwaMashu will go into meltdown now. There will be many lives lost. And an Englishman doesn't belong in the middle of this. No way."

At that point, a woman grabbed Vusi's shoulder. She was wailing, weeping. Charlie had heard the phrase "ululating" but had never really understood it until this moment. All around him, the Zulu women were ululating, issuing a high-pitched, rhythmic scream only made by a human in a severe state of emotional breakdown. An impossible sound, a deeply unpleasant noise.

But it was a rallying call too, calling the men to witness the crisis, redress the balance.

No man could sort this one out. As Charlie looked beyond Vusi and Jabu, he could see at least a dozen bodies on the floor, motionless.

Several others were jerking spasmodically, some were screaming, bloodied. It was carnage, a scene from hell.

And the woman was saying to Vusi in an hysterical mixture of Zulu, English and Afrikaans: "Your brother Vusi, he's dead, the Boere guns killed him. Dood. Deur die kop. A bullet through the head. Ai Vusi, call your mother..."

Vusi, Jabu and Charlie ran through the crowd. A small knot of youths with red bandannas had gathered around three bodies on the floor. Two were badly injured, wailing and calling for help. One lay cold, still. A small red hole smack, bang in the middle of his forehead. Vusi threw up as he ran, then reached the body of Thulane, his 15-year-old brother. He picked him up, cradled his body in his arms. Charlie could see the back of his head now. Or what was left of it. The police must have been using the dum-dum bullets he'd read about in the mafiosa novels. Mercury filled. Small entry site, horrific exit wound. He didn't have a chance.

Charlie dragged himself away from Vusi's grief. He turned to the other two lads. One was clearly on his way out. The bullet had entered his chest, ripping out most of one lung as it passed through his body.

The other had taken a bullet through the bicep. Tomato soup. Squirting out of the wound. Like nothing Charlie had ever seen before. Without thinking, he stripped off his shirt. His years in the Boy Scouts had taught him a little first aid. Tourniquets. He tied the shirt firmly around the upper arm. The blood flow slowed to a drip. The guy was fitting too, jerking and jumping. Charlie stuck his hand in the guy's mouth, holding down his tongue, hoping he was doing the right thing, hoping he wouldn't lose a finger.

The gathering crowd around them closed in, shouting, screaming. Then the wounded boy relaxed, stopped screaming. Charlie shouted: "Water, bring me water!" A big woman reached forward with a plastic bottle. Charlie put a drop on his tongue. "You can't drink too much, lad, you might need an operation later."

The crowd began to drop back, trusting the Englishman in their midst. Vusi came and squatted beside him. "We must get you out, Charlie. The cops will kill you if they come back for another go."

"I'm not leaving this boy until he gets treatment, Vusi."

Jabu came up. He looked at Vusi's contorted face. The township would be in flames later. There were 14 dead, eight severely injured, two more likely to die. And probably 30 winged by the flying rounds of the Trojan Horse soldiers. And Vusi's brother, one of 12 from his highly-political clan, would not be a loss suffered easily among the agitators in the township tonight.

"Charlie, come on, you can't stay here…"

A truck pulled up, pushing through the crowd. White men with guns. "What's happening here, mense, people?" asked the Afrikaner, in a white safari suit, their non-uniform, a lightweight matching jacket and trousers. "Trouble?"

The crowd were barely controllable. Jabu offered: "The soldiers shot these people, we need ambulances baas."

"No, no, boy," said the Afrikaner, "These people are beyond help. And it couldn't have been our soldiers. Do you hear me? We don't shoot civilians."

Charlie stood up. His patient was breathing, calm. "I'm an Englishman. I play football here. I saw them do it. Two truckloads of uniformed soldiers with automatic rifles. They hid behind the boxes, then opened fire on women and children indiscriminately. This is a serious crime sir."

The Afrikaner's eyes narrowed. "And who the vok do you think you are Englishman, to say that to a member of the Government? Bosman, arrest this man!"

A second white man, carrying a pistol, came forward. He had hand-cuffs. "I'm a British citizen, you cannot arrest me for telling the truth..." started Charlie.

"Sonny, you're not British here, you're a criminal. No white men are permitted in the township without a permit. You're in deep shit, Englishman."

It was said with finality. Jabu and Vusi had melted away, the mob had backed off. Dead and dying laying littering the street, and they were arresting him, wasting time while lives could be saved.

Then, mercifully, the sound of sirens. Many sirens. The Afrikaner showed him a badge. It said: "Inspektor Louis Moolman, Bureau of State Security." So this guy was from BOSS. The South African secret police, so adept at helping troublesome folk disappear in Apartheid South Africa. Equally good at preventing any real information about their particular style of repression escaping into the international media.

Which is why, when a female American voice rang out, Louis Moolman was stopped in his tracks. "Hey, Louis, am I allowed to film any of this," shouted a slim, attractive white woman with a cameraman in tow. "Looks like a helluva story. How are you going to explain this one?"

Moolman turned, furious. "I've told you before woman, the NBC are not allowed to film in the townships without permission. Get back in that van and go!"

"It's not a van, Louis, it's an ambulance. Only way I could get through the road-blocks, sorry. They've got work to do."

Charlie stooped and picked up his injured youth. He gently carried him towards the first of three ambulances.

The five heavily-armed BOSS agents and the angry black mob parted for him. Charlie carried the boy on through the back doors. They shut quickly behind him… Jabu and Vusi were both inside. Jabu banged on the cab. They shot off, away from the carnage, the surreal, awful reality of South Africa. And the BOSS agents, desperately trying to get the American woman's cameras turned off.

CHAPTER 4: RESETTLING:

"The pants of today are better than the breeches of tomorrow."

Moore proverb (Burkina Faso)

CHARLIE spent the Ambulance journey trying to keep his patient on the stretcher in the back as the driver hurled his vehicle through the streets to the motorway.

Vusi was beyond tears. He was sullen, angry. Jabu murmured in his ear. Vusi said: "One day, Induna, you'll realise. We have to do something now. This is enough..."

Charlie instinctively reached out a hand. Vusi didn't react at first. Then he gripped the Englishman, hard. "Thank you Charlie, I think you might have saved Joshua. He would have bled to death. You're not like the others man. Why do white men think they can shoot us for throwing stones? For demanding our rights?

"In this country we are the aliens. You've been here a week and you can go where you want, do what you want. We have lived here for generations and we are treated like strangers in our own lands. Migrants allowed to work in this country, but not allowed to enjoy the fruits of our labour."

Charlie looked at Vusi. "You talk like a university lecturer Vusi. One day your people will be free. I'm going to tell everyone what I have seen here today. This can't go on. Like the Nazis couldn't go on in Germany. I'll tell the truth, they'll listen to an Englishman."

Jabu grunted: "If you ever get to talk in public again. The BOSS guys will be after you Charlie, mark my words. All I wanted was a centre-forward, not a fucking hero. A quiet life, a League title, that's all I was after."

Vusi looked at Jabu, shook his head: "You old guys think it's fine to live under this system. Live within it. But I'm telling you man, we have to have change or the whole place will become a killing field."

They sat quietly. Charlie mopped Joshua's forehead, wiped the blood from his arm, which had gone an alarming shade of blue beneath the makeshift tourniquet.

There was another wound in his calf and another bullet had creased his temple, leaving a deep furrow which leaked thick, red blood. If Joshua survived this, he was a cat with three lives down.

The hospital, ironically, was also called the Princess Magogo. It sat nestled at the top of the Berea, above the expensive slope of mansions rising up out of the hub of Durban along the highway which pointed towards Pietermaritzburg.

The area at the top of the Berea was balanced between the white and Asian zones, carefully demarcated by the Urban Areas Act of 1961. Overport was almost a cross-over zone. The black hospital provided a natural boundary.

A white doctor, barely 20, was standing at the back of the ambulance. "I'm Piet," he said to Charlie, ignoring Jabu and Vusi, "I hear there's been a shooting."

"A shooting?" Charlie shook his head, "A bloody massacre. You'll be taking bodies all night. But I think we can save Joshua here. Three wounds, right bicep, left calf and there... the right temple."

Piet, a national serviceman doing his houseman year in a military uniform in a black hospital, had not had the best of days. It was a nightmare job. Not like a trainee medical doctor anywhere in the rest of the world might expect.

The rule was: Any young black women should be sterilised, no matter what the problem. Any young black men with bullet wounds should be reported to Inspektor Moolman.

But Piet had attended the Witwatersrand University medical school. Wits was a haven for left-wing thinking in Johannesburg and though most medical students were inherently conservative, Piet Vermeulen was a footballer and cricketer, he understood fair play. And he recognised a fellow sportsman in this English lad.

"So, how did you get involved in all this, mate?" he asked, "Best stay out of the townships when it's all going mad."

"I was just on my way to football training, Piet," said Charlie. "The cops hid in a truck behind boxes and when the kids started throwing stones, they just opened fire. It was disgusting. Like fucking Apocalypse Now. Something has to be done. You can't just shoot women and kids because a gang of teenagers is throwing stones."

"Bricks, more like," said Piet, his South African education preventing him from agreeing too wholeheartedly with the Englishman, "But I take your point. It's an over-reaction."

He was examining Joshua's wounds. He looked up at Jabu and Vusi. "Either of you guys his dad?" he asked, "Whoever tied this tourniquet saved this boy's life."

Jabu put a hand on Charlie's shoulder. Vusi said quietly: "He's a friend. My brother was killed tonight. I hope they'll bring the body in soon. I need to see him once more."

Vusi sobbed then, deep, racking sobs. Piet stood up. "This boy will be okay, I'll see to him. I'm sorry for your loss my friend."

Vusi looked up, saw only Piet's brown uniform. "Yeah, I bet you are."

Charlie visited the hospital the next morning, after a restless night in his hotel, waiting for a late-night call from the Inspektor which never came.

Piet was still there. He was on a 72-hour shift. And the last eight hours had consisted of issuing death certificates as the bodies were brought in from KwaMashu.

"Look, I'll tell you okay. This is bullshit. Nobody has ever done this before. Shooting like this. It's the start of something very, very bad. But if you say anything, if I say anything, you'll disappear. Take it from me Charlie, keep your mouth shut, take the next flight out of here.

"God, I wish I was in London doing my houseman year. Proper medicine, the NHS, funding, everyone treated the same. Not this shit. They expect me to sterilise the black women, report the black men if they are wounded. Patient confidentiality? Human rights? Bollocks!"

Charlie gave Joshua as much money as he had on him. He'd seen the white guys outside the ward. Moustaches. BOSS. He whispered to Joshua: "Good luck lad, get a taxi home. They're after me, those guys."

Joshua had recovered quickly under Piet's ministrations. He grabbed Charlie. "No, don't leave me, they'll take me. I'll disappear."

With that, remarkably given his wounds, Joshua leapt up in his surgical gown. Without thinking, Charlie wrapped a towel around him and headed for the toilets. The two of them opened the window and dropped down onto the tarmac.

They walked to the narrow side road, no police cars in sight.

Charlie saw the taxi driver who had driven him up to the hospital. "Take this guy to KwaMashu, wherever he wants to go, quick," the driver nodded, taking the bundle of notes. Joshua waved and left. Charlie would never see him again. Would never know what happened to his other six lives.

He took a bus back into the city, had lunch, tried to think straight. And Jabu was there to pick him up for training.

"It's on," said Jabu, "The cops are everywhere. Nobody can move in KwaMashu. But they've asked me to keep the football going. It keeps the people calm, makes things seem normal. What can I do?"

They were waved through the roadblocks. No problem. Training was weird. Like nothing had happened. Even The Prof didn't want to talk about it. Right at the end, he took Charlie aside and said: "I've heard all about what you did. What you saw. Keep quiet. Things are bad. Bide your time. There will be a time and place for the truth, but now it's only going to cost you your life."

Merv and Andy drove Charlie home, talking blithely about the rumours of shootings the night before. "I heard they shot 30 agitators last night," said Merv, "Blerrie good thing too. Bloody kaffirs."

Charlie decided it wasn't worth arguing with Merv. Not now. Not ever, probably. In his mind, all he could see were bullets flying, women and children torn apart. A wounded teenager in hospital scarred for life, scared for his life. A doctor told to stop the natives reproducing. Doctors tying off women's tubes or injecting them with three-month contraceptive chemicals with a reputation for causing cancer. Shit, a week in Africa and he had no grip on reality any more.

He was on the gin the minute he hit the hotel. Andy stayed for a while, Charlie told him what he had seen. Andy went quiet. "Fuck." Then: "Best you don't tell anybody else what you saw. They'll ban you. They did that to a journalist bloke I knew. He couldn't be in a room with more than one other person at any time, even at home. He had to report to the police every day. Wasn't allowed to leave his house without permission. His phone was bugged. Like bloody house arrest only much worse. Just forget it, we need you to stay until the end of the season. Big win bonuses son, let's just get on with it."

Charlie thought about the big angry outburst at that point but again... what was the point? He would bide his time, tell the truth when it mattered. When it might make a difference.

Andy left with Charlie halfway through his third gin. The pretty barmaid called him over. "Phone call for Burton!" she smiled, gloriously.

"Charlie, it's Vusi," said an indistinct voice, "I want you to come to Thulane's funeral. It will be a big show, tomorrow. I'll pick you up at 11. The people know what you did for Joshua... and how you got him out when BOSS were waiting. Good job. We go on playing football, we bide our time Charlie. Are you with us?"

"More than ever Vusi," said Charlie, and the phone went dead. Then, just as he was about to put the receiver down, another click. Quiet, but distinct.

The cemetery at KwaMashu was fascinating. More money had been spent here than anywhere else in the township. Death meant a lot to the Zulus. They would pay thousands for a good funeral, a proper service, a marble gravestone. Like British people in medieval times, thought Charlie, remembering the Parish Church in Fareham, filled with expensive grave-stones and cheap suits.

He stood next to Jabu and the rest of the team, minus Andy and Merv. They were all in green tracksuits, Henry Cele, the regal goalkeeper, held a Royals flag high.

Hundreds of mourners were gathering. Then a low singing and, over the hill, a vast mob of angry young teenagers. "They're toy-toying," said Jabu, "They're angry. We just watch."

Several youths led the way, dancing with a strange, spasmodic rhythm. They sang with a soulful lilt. Charlie had never seen a funeral like this. Never imagined a death could be commemorated this way. There was sadness, joy, anger, acceptance… and more anger. And music, and dancing, and shooting. A group of youths in red bandannas stood over the coffin. They raised AK47 rifles, and fired three times into the air.

Then they sang a strange, beautiful song. "That's Nkosi Sikelele," explained Jabu, "It's the National Anthem really. The Afrikaners have another anthem, but this is the people's song. Nkosi Sikele means "God bless Africa" and if the police hear you sing it, you will be shot!"

"It's beautiful, Jabu," said Charlie, "This whole thing is incredible, moving. I've never seen anything like it."

Then "Mad Eyes" Dlamini appeared. He did a dance uncannily similar to the one he'd done celebrating Charlie's first goal on Sunday. Then he spoke. Though it was all in Zulu, Charlie could sense what he was saying from the rise and fall of his tone, the urgency of his gesticulations. He was telling them that Thulane and Lukas – the boy whose lungs had been shot away – were fine boys, young warriors, who deserved to die with pride. They had died serving their people, seeking freedom. With stones and bricks. Before they were shot by dum-dum bullets.

Charlie found himself crying by the time the more traditional preacher spoke. Then a tall Zulu in a fine suit emerged from a huge black BMW, bearded and obviously a leader, he stood and said in English through a megaphone: "These boys were our future. The Boere have taken them away with machine guns. God will give us strength. God will be there to judge the men who raised those guns. We have lost 16 innocent lives. May God forgive them, may God bring justice."

And then he shouted: "AMANDLA" and the thousands standing in the cemetery and beyond responded "AWETHU". "Power" Jabu explained, "To the people."

And then the helicopter swooped low over their heads, trailing a thick stream of smoking tear gas. The huge crowd stood firm. Then the fumes began to bite. Charlie felt his nose sting. Then his throat began to close. His arm-pits stung. The crowd erupted and ran. Just as the sirens began to wail on the road outside. Chaos. Baton-charging policemen in riot gear, more gun-fire, big, steep-sided vehicles specially designed for dealing with street crowds, driving straight into the fleeing mourners.

As Charlie ran behind Jabu and his team-mates, he spied men in white safari suits. With revolvers and television cameras. Standing, watching, filming. Half a mile further on, there was the American woman, doing exactly the same.

Chaos. Then, finally, a bus. The Royals poured in. And retired to the Shebeen.

Vusi joined them. He had been one of the gunmen in the red bandannas. He was angry, but his eyes were shining: "I think I got one, one of those fucking BOSS bastards!"

The shebeen erupted. "I shot him, like this," said Vusi, striking a child-like shooting pose, and shouting "Kerpow!" "The Boer went down. Dead! Amandla!"

The shebeen replied with a hearty "Awethu" from the people, yet strangely Charlie didn't feel excluded. Vusi sat beside him. Quietly, he whispered: "I know you saved Joshua. He is safe. We've sent him to Zambia. You are a good man. But if the crowd take you Englishman, I can't help you. Please go. I don't want you hurt. And this isn't a good place for whiteys right now."

Charlie nodded. "I know Vusi. And I appreciate that. But I ain't leaving. I owe it to Jabu to stay. I owe it to you to stay. We'll win everything, then I go home and tell the world what I've seen. That's how we play it."

Vusi turned, looked deep into his eyes. "You serious? This is the real world man, not a fucking game. BOSS will disappear you long before the end of the season."

"No Vusi, I've got an English passport. They can't touch me. The consulate will come to my rescue. I'm not going. I'm going to make you and your people realize some of us care, some of us are human. And one day, I'll hold my head up high and say: I did that. I wasn't part of the problem, I was part of the solution."

Vusi laughed. "You're fucking mad Englishman. But good luck. We play on Sunday like nothing's happened. We bide our time. And you'd better bloody score!"

As it happened, he did. Only once this time, but it was enough to win his first home game in front of nearly 20,000 packed into the Princess Magogo that Sunday against African Wanderers, the side from Hammarsdale, a particularly tough area just outside neighbouring Pietermaritzburg.

They won 2-0, Andy got the other with a trade-mark towering header in the "psychologically crucial" period just before half-time.

But that was after another Burton Beauty, as the Mercury described it after their weekly chat with Clive Fox. Charlie had turned the centre-back on the edge of the box and curled one in the top corner after about 25 minutes.

In celebration he had lifted his shirt over his head – revealing a picture of Thulane on a black vest with RIP emblazoned upon it. No idea where he got the idea from, he'd got a shop in Durban to make it up despite the strange looks. Risky, but Charlie had felt it was the right thing to do… and he saw plenty of examples of that sort of thing later in his life. Football provided a stage, a spotlight. And sometimes you had to use it.

Though Vusi and the fans loved it, Jabu was furious, taking him off at half-time and berating him for drawing attention to himself. Charlie had spent the rest of the weekend and the early part of the week in a "safe-house" – Merv's unheated wendy house, with two large Alsatians, former police dogs. Friendly enough. If you weren't black. Even the police dogs were racist here.

And now it was a midweek away game against Port Elizabeth outfit, Bayi United. The team travelled in a bus, but Jabu sent the white guys off in a separate car to avoid trouble at the road blocks. The Royals were up to second in the table – slotting neatly between Chiefs and Pirates – though they hadn't trained properly for a week.

Port Elizabeth was a major trek. Given that black men rarely flew on the domestic flights between the major South Africa cities, such drives were common for sides in the NPL.

And then there was the homelands question. To travel through the "independent" nations of the Transkei and Ciskei, putting up with passport control points and corrupt fledgling police enforcing imaginary speed limits – or zip around the outside via Kokstad, cutting in to make the trip nearly 1,000 miles rather than a coastal adventure of around 800?

In the end they chose some kind of convoluted route which took them all over the place. Down a winding road through the beautiful South Coast resorts, where he passed, bizarrely Margate, Ramsgate, St Michael's Bay and Ilfracombe (pronounced Ill Frack Combi) by Merv. Then they cut around the newly-built casino and golf course at Wild Coast, just beyond Port Shepstone... and left civilisation behind.

The Transkei was the oldest of the homelands, a bizarre set of fragmented countries throughout South Africa where the National Party Government intended to house their black majority. And, in a brilliant demographic twist, eventually all blacks would carry the passports of these tiny nations, where they could vote and live.

Of course, it was a deeply floored policy. But they were spending gazillions of rand to make it work. Bvenda and Bophuthatswana in the north, KwaZulu spotted all over Natal and here, in the Eastern Cape where the Xhosa had lived for years, the tribe of Nelson Mandela were supposed to live in the Transkei and neighbouring Ciskei, venturing out as migrant labourers to work in South Africa.

As Vusi had so often said, it was as if the indigenous people were aliens in their own land. Oh, the homelands were a lovely excuse for the Government. They put up a couple of passport checkpoints on the major roads, they built casinos, night clubs and soft-porn cinemas and the white tourists flocked to the Wild Coast and Sun City to do all the things they weren't allowed to do by the dominant Dutch Reformed Church in mainland South Africa.

Problem was, the land gifted to the homelands wasn't historically the home of these tribes. It was a sham. The plan was to house around eighty percent of the population of South Africa in about twenty percent of the land, carefully chosen shards of hopeless, empty scrubland. Historians attempted to suggest these were the traditional tribal areas and the real clincher? Anybody speaking the language of a certain tribe found without a "passbook" which showed he had a job in the "white" cities were simply bundled up and driven off to their particular homeland to eke out an existence in a bleak shanty town hundreds of miles away without electricity or running water, established schools or churches.

That was the plan. Charlie tried to discuss the whole homelands strategy with Andy and Merv, but they didn't get far. Merv grunted: "It's the best place for the kaffirs. If they haven't got a job in the city, send them back to their homeland. Let the Sothos go to Lesotho and the Swazis can piss off to Swaziland..."

"But Merv," argued Charlie, "Lesotho and Swaziland don't want South Africa's unemployed. They're British protectorates granted independence within South Africa's borders years ago."

"Okay then," said Merv, toeing the National Party line, "Put the Sothos in that bit next to Lesotho, put the Xhosas in the Transkei and Ciskei... get them out. And then we can go play golf for the weekend, gamble a bit, watch the blue movies. It's a great idea man; these guys, Pik Vermeulen and PW Vermeulen, they're guided by God, I'm telling you.

"Who else could have thought of something like this? Separate nations, separate development. And one day all the blacks will have their own little country according to their tribe. They all hate each other anyway."

"No Merv, it's a divide-and-rule policy," said Charlie, growing frustrated by the one-eyed Afrikaner, "The truth is all the black guys have the same political aspirations. One man, one vote, one nation, one South Africa under Mandela."

Andy winced. "Shit, Charlie, you sound like one of those Communists. You talk like that and you'll get arrested under the Suppression of Communism act. And you won't be putting your boots on again for a while."

"But how can you expect to pack people off to the bush, pretend they've got a country... when they've got nothing? And all the mines and farms and cities are in the white bit? The big, rich bit?"

Merv was growing angry now. "Charlie, it works for us, okay? Don't question it. You've been here a couple of weeks, seen a bit of shit. But really, it's a great country. We beat the blacks when we ran away from the British in the Cape Colony in the 1830s. The Great Trek... what do you know about that?

"You know how brave those guys were? Taking on Chaka and the Zulus away from home? And, thanks to God, we won. It's how it's going to be. And when the British tried to take the land off us in the Boer Wars, with Lord Kitchener's concentration camps, we fought ourselves to a standstill."

"Yup, and we won. But I wish we hadn't," said Charlie, "What we did was as bad as what you guys are doing to the blacks now. We made you second class citizens, you Afrikaners. And then when we all went off to fight the second World War, the Afrikaners supported the Nazis and after the war, you had taken over the SABC and all the important organizations… and you voted Jan Smuts out in the 1948 elections, just like Winston Churchill in England.

"Smuts helped win the war against the Nazis, but the people at home turned on him."

Merv was surprised by Charlie's brief but accurate history of the Afrikaner's rise to power, supported by the Hitler-supporting Ossewa Brandwag (Ox-wagon Home Guard) and a shadowy Masonic organization known as the Broederbond (Brotherhood). They had quietly loosened the grip of the British in South Africa… then grabbed power in 1948. By 1961 they had shuffled the electoral boundaries around to suit the rural Afrikaners and the Union became a Republic. They declared their 'Republiek' in 1961 and set about realising Hendrik Verwoerd's Apartheid dream, separate development involving schools, urban areas, mixed marriages, homelands. It took all their resources to make it work. Anybody who opposed the National Party or called for a state which looked after the impoverished became a Communist; censorship was encouraged, naked women were as illegal as pictures of Mandela since his life-sentence had commenced in 1963. Ironically, the only real political opposition came from the right, the Hereformeede Nasionale Party, the reformed nationalists, who felt the government were being too nice to the blacks. Verwoerd had been assassinated by an immigrant who felt that way.

Apartheid (pronounced, ironically apart-hate) was, to Merv and the average Afrikaner, a work of God-given genius, especially when you looked north at Kenneth Kaunda's Zambia, Julius Nyerere's Tanzania, Hastings Banda's Malawi and, most recently, Robert Mugabe's Zimbabwe. All one-party states, all falling apart, like

Mozambique and Angola since the Portuguese had left in 1970. And once, under white rule, they had been happy, economically-viable nations. To listen to the white economists, the state of the southern African nations was the best possible argument for Apartheid.

The bit Merv and his buddies didn't mention was South Africa's role in de-stabilising their neighbours. Merv himself had been in a military operation in Angola three years before, part of a convoy so big he couldn't see the front of it, nor the back. While the South African Defence Force were supposed to be protecting their borders against Cuban-backed insurgent groups to the north, they actually went as far as the north-Angolan oil-rich enclave of Cabinda to disrupt production... and to the Mozambique-Zimbabwe oil pipelines at Beira, where Merv's mate had gone ashore from an e-boat and blown the place apart. Still, as Merv would always argue, all's fair in love and war, especially when you're fighting the coons.

The only problem about this bloody Homelands policy? The border patrols. They either wanted money in your ID book... or they were job's-worth idiots who wouldn't let you through without the correct paperwork.

And Charlie clearly didn't have the right paperwork. He hadn't realized he'd need his British passport to get to Port Elizabeth. They had breezed through either side of the Transkei via a ragged capital city called Umtata, thanks to a few useful bribes. But here, at the entrance to the Ciskei, the uniformed border guards weren't letting the Englishman through. No way. No money would do it. Charlie was a foreigner going nowhere fast.

Merv and Andy were stumped. They didn't want to hang about here, where a gang of troublesome blacks could suddenly emerge out of the bush to take the six-cylinder, souped-up Cortina with fat tyres and go-faster stripes.

"Look, Charlie, you can hitch-hike man, no trouble," said Andy,

"I know it doesn't happen in Britain anymore, but here it's encouraged for white guys to pick up people thumbing a lift. It helps the National Servicemen get home from duty."

Charlie was astounded. "What? You're going to leave me here and drive off to Port Elizabeth? Where do I go?"

"Head for Kokstad," said Merv helpfully, "Then down to PE. It won't be difficult. If you get stuck, call the Holiday Inn at Summerstrand, we'll be there in about five hours. Jabu will send somebody out to get you."

And with that, Merv and Andy drove off, leaving Charlie alone at the checkpoint. The great African adventure had suddenly gone wrong. Merv and Andy didn't like his conversation, sure. They thought he was a trouble-maker. But leaving him here…?

Charlie walked across the Fish River, a huge watery highway into the Ciskei. A few cars drove the other way. A truck went past heading towards Kokstad… and Charlie held out a thumb. Nothing. Then another. And another.

Finally, a Volkswagen beetle, so popular in South Africa, scuttled past… and pulled over when his thumb went up.

Charlie ran forward, pulled open the passenger door.

He instantly wished he hadn't. The black face that greeted him was a horror mask. The nose had been spit, recently, and badly stitched. Black marks on his forehead and his cheeks. One ear bandaged. Teeth broken and missing.

"Hey man, jump in, where you going?" the guy asked. "You don't want to wait around here, the cops will be all over you. Or the bad guys, the Tsotsi's will have those boots."

Charlie looked down. His football boots were clutched in his arm. He'd nearly forgotten. He climbed in, clearly hesitant.

The driver put out a hand, Charlie shook it. Looking at that face again. Fascinated. "Oh, this," said the driver, "The cops did that. Nothing a bit of cosmetic surgery can't fix when I'm rich!"

They roared off in the little Volkswagen. Silence. Charlie broke it: "I'm Charlie Burton, I'm over here from England, playing football for the Chaka Royals…"

"Usuthu!" the driver responded, laughing, "I'm a Pirates fan myself. Come from Joburg. The name's Poti, Nkosana Poti. I'm afraid we'll have to stay away from the border crossings. I'm heading for Port Elizabeth, a meeting…"

"Brilliant," said Charlie, "The rest of the team are on their way to the Holiday Inn at Summerstrand, we're playing Bayi tomorrow…"

"No problem man, I'll get you there. As long as we don't get stopped. No passbook I'm afraid… I'm an illegal I guess."

"Me too," said Charlie, more relaxed. This bloke was easy to talk to. And they talked as they drove along a strange road with various signs saying: "You are now entering KwaZulu" and "You are now leaving KwaZulu" then "You are now entering Ciskei" and rapidly "You are now leaving Ciskei".

Charlie joked about the homeland system, about the fragmented country he was just starting to know. Nkosana had plenty to say on the subject. And it was nothing like Merv's line of argument.

Nkosana was 23, a leader in something called the Pan Africanist Congress. He was a revolutionary, to the left even of the banned African National Congress of Mandela and Tambo. And he was proud of it.

"See these scars," he asked Charlie, "The cops in John Vorster Square, the police headquarters in Johannesburg. They take people in, torture them, find out who their friends are, torture you some more, then drop you out of a window. You think I'm joking…"

"No," said Charlie earnestly, "I've watched stuff about South Africa on the BBC in England. I believe you… and I've seen some things in a few days here…"

He told Nkosana about the Trojan Horse massacre, the cops on the beachfront, the tear-gas at the funeral.

Nkosana listened intently. "I've heard about these things, the cops are stepping up the pressure. Soon the National Servicemen won't be on the border, they'll be in the townships, keeping the peace with automatic weapons and grenades, not their sjamboks (long, whip-like leather canes) and tear gas like the police.

"We'll never be free in our own land. We will always be the enemy."

They'd been driving for a while now, somehow slipping through the Ciskei without papers on the back roads. They were on a dirt track, with the occasional clump of ramshackle corrugated iron shacks popping up on the side of the road.

Charlie was asking how they moved people to the Ciskei and the other homelands. Nkosana said: "They started by clearing the multi-racial suburbs. Places like District Six in Cape Town, Sofia Town in Johannesburg. Black and white, coloured and Indian, we all lived next to each other in places like that. We could be friends, we could talk, listen to jazz together, play football… the National Party didn't like that, it didn't fit in with their great plan.

"So they bull-dozed the "grey" areas and had to find a place for the displaced people. Then they had to get rid of the squatter camps near the cities, put their Urban Areas Act into practice. And they'd simply send in the security forces, knock it all down, and bus the people off to places like this."

He looked at Charlie, looked around himself at the barren landscape dotted with shacks. "You look like an Englishman who cares," he said, "You want to see something not many people get to see? Hey, you look a bit black anyway… you're lucky you didn't grow up here, they'd have been putting a pencil in your hair to see if you're black…"

Charlie muttered something about his dad being from Burundi, but then Nkosana turned down a smaller dirt track, along a curving road around a hill… and behind it, a huge squatter camp emerged in the open veldt.

Downhill from the shacks lay a brown, brackish lake. A small brick church stood in the middle of it all, but there were no other permanent buildings Charlie could see.

"A resettlement camp," Nkosana said, turning up his battered nose at the smell, "These people are the ones I'm talking about. Taken from the city and dumped here with a few possessions for the Ciskei government to look after. In reality, they've been abandoned. No money, no food, no farms, no nothing."

They climbed out of the car. If KwaMashu had been a bit of a culture shock, this was far, far worse.

No merry shouting or kicking of tennis balls here. The few people he could see looked listless, sick. And dreadfully thin. Though it was winter and less than tropical, they didn't have a proper coat between them.

"This is what the Nationalists don't want the world to see," said Nkosana, "And there are millions living like this all over South Africa in the so-called homelands. It's disgusting. And nobody is doing anything about it."

Charlie could barely believe his eyes. Somebody had tried to build a school of sorts on the side of the camp. It stood empty, abandoned, with a few desks and broken blackboards visible through the open doorways.

A few old men wandered around, tiny children ran up to Charlie, begging for "ten cents for bread", though one wanted a cigarette, if he'd heard him right.

Nkosana kept close, watching the Englishman's face. Seeing his shock. Some of the kids were painfully thin, with open sores, snotty noses, bandy legs indicating serious malnutrition that was beyond treatment.

They were drawn to the brick church. A few starving children were moving in and out of the open doors. A pregnant woman was slumped against a wall. There were no men: "all off trying to get work in Uitenhage at the car factories" explained Nkosana.

Charlie entered the building. Not so much a church as a drab, brick house with a cross on the top. No frills. Inside, pandemonium. Sick children filled every inch of the concrete floor. Covered by blankets and towels, an open fire burned in the grate but it failed to disguise the stink of faeces and vomit. Charlie wanted to turn and run. A white woman appeared on the far side of the room. She looked exhausted, stooped by the burden that lay helpless between them… 30 children obviously hovering on the edge of the abyss.

The woman looked 60 from a distance, but as Charlie made his way towards her, carefully stepping over children with hacking, adult coughs, he could see she was closer to 30, yet worn-out by whatever she was doing here.

"Welcome," she said, "It's good to see you. How can you help us?"

Charlie was taken aback. "I don't know love, we just drove up and found all this. What's happened here? Has there been an attack? An epidemic?"

"No, no, it's always like this," she replied, with a tinkling laugh, "I've been here two years and this is about the quietest our clinic has been. I thought you were a visitor with funds…."

"Oh," said Charlie, reaching into his wallet and extracting everything in it, "I've got something, but you need the bloody United Nations, the World Health Organisation, not my money…"

"I know," she said, ignoring his language "But the authorities won't let anybody near here. And we are the only medical facility in 50 miles for these people. They've been left here to die. We can't just leave them."

She spoke quietly as she moved among the children, quieting them, soothing them, trying desperately to bring a smile to their tiny, pain-racked faces.

Charlie had never seen anything like this. Malnourished and sick, it looked like none of these children, all under five, would survive the night. Of course, some would; but many would never have a normal life after their time in the resettlement camp, their mothers starving, their fathers miles away in a desperate search for money which usually ended with a night in jail because they didn't have a stamped passbook.

Without any kind of infrastructure, no farms or shops nearby, these people had been left to rot. The woman, Sister Michaela, was from a band of nuns in Austria. By chance they had put a mission here twenty years ago, before the resettlement camps. And their tiny brick clinic had attracted more and more squatters looking for help.

In the old days, she explained, there had been farm trucks selling fruit and vegetables at the side of the road. The people had been able to drink from the lake and use the river for cleaning. But as more and more jobless, homeless Xhosas were "resettled" the farmers had become reluctant to get too close for fear of being mobbed, the lake had become polluted and disease had spread rapidly in the past two years.

Michaela and two other nuns, both currently in a state of exhausted sleep, did their best to maintain some sort of medical facility running, with occasional visits from well-meaning Europeans. But now even they were being stopped by the authorities from coming near. And a new disease, a nasty bug which attacked the immune system called AIDS, was sweeping through the local populace, adding to the problems of malnourishment, rickets and influenza.

"To be honest, Mr Burton, I don't know how much longer we can carry on here without real help," said Sister Michaela, "But if any of the three of us leave, the whole system will break down, and dozens will die. They cut off the telephone six months ago, since then it's been getting worse and worse. Can you bring help from England? Anywhere...?"

As they moved through the five patient-packed rooms of the clinic, Charlie and Nkosana were stunned by the cheerfulness Michaela showed in the face of man-made death.

Two small children rushed up as they entered a room full of pregnant women. There must have been 20 of them, several screaming, lying on bloodied blankets. The sisters delivered "five or six" a week, but lost "two or three".

The two infants – clearly twins, though not identical, one was a boy, the other a girl - pulled Charlie over to a small bundle on the floor. They looked up at his face, eyes wide. They must have been four at the most. The girl was beautiful, clear skin, chubby, vibrant. The boy was taller, serious, all skin and bone. Charlie leaned over the bundle and pulled a blanket back. Flies were buzzing around the face of the tiny woman curled up under the blanket.

She was barely alive. She spoke quietly to the twins. Michaela walked over quickly. "Mr Burton, best not get too close there, it's this AIDS thing. We don't know how contagious it is. She's not got long. She lost a child this week. Her husband hasn't been seen for six months. I don't know what to do with these two, they are so lovely."

The twins pulled at Charlie's clothes again, giggling, chattering. Nkosana smiled. "They're saying you are Father Christmas, Charlie. Their mother's told them God sent you from a long way away to look after them and bring them presents."

Nkosana bent over the stricken woman. The smell was nearly overpowering. The twins' mother, nameless, muttered something brief. Gave a small cry. And went quiet. Everything went quiet.

Charlie knew in his heart what had happened. Nkosana stood up slowly. He looked at Charlie, curious: "She said you'd look out for her children and... and then she said your dad was from Abidjan. I think she was delirious. She's gone now."

Nkosana had seen plenty of shit in his life. Growing up in Alexandria, an older and even tougher Johannesburg township than Soweto, he had seen plenty of death, plenty of orphans. But now he saw the tears in Charlie's eyes, the oblivious twins hoping for a play-mate, Sister Michaela moving towards them, knowing what had happened to their mother. And Nkosana cried too. For his people, for this place, for the people who caused nightmare moments like these.

Then, amid the sobs, the other sound of Africa. A siren. Sister Michaela could cope with death. Not the local police, who had twice raped her. "Somebody has betrayed you. They've run to the police station and told them there's an Englishman in the camp. They get a rand for that. You must go. The police are cruel to me, but they will kill you for what you have seen here today."

Nkosana pulled Charlie away from the twins and their dead mother. Sister Michaela, her shoulders slumped in hopelessness, watched them go, saying a quick prayer before turning to begin the process of burial, her third that day.

Charlie and Nkosana ran for the Volkswagen. The cop van had stopped on the far side of the camp, across the stinking lake. They released a dog. And then another. "Oh, shit!" shouted Nkosana, "Run Charlie, run."

The four white policemen were laughing. In no rush. They knew the carefully-trained Alsatians would do their job, stop them, bring these two down in the bare ground between the shacks and the road. You needed a permit to leave the tarmac roads in the Eastern Cape. Resettlement camps like this were not for public consumption. And the BOSS agents would be along once they had these two in the cells. They couldn't be allowed to leave now, not after what they'd seen in that tiny clinic. They probably had cameras. It would be like another Ethiopia, a new Biafra if this got out.

The dogs ran fast around the lake, growling, salivating. Nkosana was running at full tilt, but he knew he'd never make it. He'd been had by a police dog once before. He'd lost most of his right calf muscle.

Charlie was running too. Then he checked. He had no idea why. His experience with dogs was limited to dealing with the yapping, annoying mongrels who interrupted his runs around Fareham. He had a way of dealing with them, he'd seen it on a film once.

Charlie turned. His mind was cluttered by all he'd just witnessed. Death, malnutrition, desperation. Two tiny children orphaned in a moment.

So a dog didn't really matter. Two dogs mattered even less. Charlie went down on one knee. The Alsatians, snarling, vicious, charged at him. Charlie began to whistle. A low, monotonous whistle. Then a sudden high-pitched burst. The dogs were 10 yards away. Once the pitch of Charlie's whistle changed, they both checked, as if they'd hit a wall.

Charlie was eye-ball to eye-ball with them. He didn't see the saliva, the teeth, the wild eyes. He saw two unhappy hounds, eager for affection like most other mammals around these parts.

He lifted a hand, and the whistle went slowly from high to low as he arm dropped. The dogs were captivated. Their training was forgotten. Their awful need to clamp human appendages in their strong jaws appeared to have left them.

They wandered up to Charlie, tails wagging eagerly. Charlie stood, rubbed them both behind the ears. He gave them hotel front-desk sweet, slightly dusty, from his pocket. The coppers across the other side of the lake finally realised what was happening. They tried shouting encouragement at the dogs... then reached inside their jackets for weapons.

Nkosana yelled: "Charlie, hurry. Quick!" He threw more sweets at the dogs and legged it to the Volkswagen. As they disappeared over the horizon, Charlie looked back to see the coppers kicking their dogs... and the dogs, frenzied, biting back. For the first time since the clinic, he smiled.

Neither of them were ready to talk about what they had seen. In many ways Charlie was in shock. Nkosana wasn't far behind. He'd expected poverty in a Ciskei resettlement camp, but nothing like what they had just witnessed. He was also worried about the police calling ahead to intercept their fleeing Volkswagen.

They talked about England, about football. Then about Alex, the dangerous but fascinating sprawl south of Joburg and how different their lives had been.

As darkness fell, they drove through Grahamstown, home of the 1820 settlers, where thousands of English soldiers had been resettled after the Napoleonic wars to provide a buffer between the whites and the natives.

And then, an hour later, they were in Port Elizabeth. Not the most beautiful coastal city in South Africa, but it wasn't bad. Even in the dark, Charlie could see the phosphorescent lines of surf marching to the beach and he felt calmed.

For the first time, he spoke of the devastation they had seen. The nightmare town-with-no-name. Nkosana grunted: "I don't know what you'd call that place. There's a big resettlement area called Sade where the people sleep on the train overnight before they go back to work. That's bad.

"But what we saw today, that's the worst I've seen. I'll be telling everyone about it at the meeting today in New Brighton. There are many revolutionaries here. They work at the car factories in Uitenhage, they have some power, some money. We will try to do something."

"Me too," said Charlie, as the beautiful white Holiday Inn building loomed out of the night, right on a perfect sandy bay just south of the city centre, "I will never forget what I saw today Nkosana. And thanks for the lift."

Nkosana scribbled a number on a scrap of paper, pressed it into his hand. "I'll see you again, Englishman," he said, and drove off.

CHAPTER 5: IMMORALITY:

"The bush in which you hide has eyes."
                    Gusii proverb (Kenya)

Jabu was mightily pleased to see Charlie when he walked in to the hotel bar, smiling. The rest of the team roared as he entered. "I've sent Merv and Andy to their rooms for leaving you like that," said Jabu, angrily. "They had no right to leave you there. We've been worried man, we even phoned the police to try find you."

"Oh, they found me," grinned Charlie, "I had a play with their pet dogs!"

Coach Fox walked over: "Good to see you Charlie, you relax now. South African people are good with hitch hikers hey?"

Charlie laughed again: "The bloke who picked me up was certainly interesting Clive, I'm learning about this country. A lot."

Clive went up to bed. They weren't playing until the next night, Wednesday.

Charlie called the guys together. "Vusi, Prof, lads. I've got something to tell you."

With that, he launched into a full, detailed account of his day. The Zulus loved a story, a well-told tale. And this one moved them to tears. Charlie wept himself as he told of the pitiful mother's death, the smiles on the faces of her unknowing twins. The hopelessness of Sister Michaela.

But they all burst into roars of approval when he told them about the dogs. The white locals frowned at the Englishman fraternizing with the Zulus in their bar, Charlie went to buy a round and found he'd given all his money to a nun somewhere in an unnamed shanty town in the middle of nowhere. He put it on his room, explained to the locals he was an English footballer... and asked them if they'd ever driven inland and seen the resettlement camps.

He was met with blank stares. "It's terrible," said Charlie, "People starving, kids nearly dead on the floor. You can't let that go on in your country, on your doorstep."

One of the Afrikaans men at the bar said: "You come here and attack our country? What about the starving in England man? The blacks from the West Indies and the way you left India in the shit?"

Charlie laughed. "In England, even the poor have a fridge and a telly. We give money to the jobless. We've got the NHS to give medical help to everyone, equally. You've got no idea. There are people dying two hours from here, they could be helped... and you do nothing."

Jabu came up, pulled him away. "I've told you Charlie, there's a time and a place for the truth. This Holiday Inn is the only one that will take us, black and white. Don't wind them up man."

Charlie looked at the Afrikaner, who was still frothing at the mouth. "Sorry mate, great country, lovely sunshine."

Coach Clive took them for a run in the bay the next morning. It was exactly a kilometer from head to head, running on the firm sand where the waves drew back. Charlie counted 400 paces for every kilometer and while the rest of the team did two lengths of the beach, he did five. Then he leapt into the surf, the black guys laughing, Merv and Andy joining him, but only going in a few feet.

Charlie was in the waves, his head underwater, when he heard a squeaking, high-pitched noise. He lifted his head. Dolphin, about 30 yards off, leaping in the breakers. Without a second thought, Charlie swam out to them, catching the waves as he'd learned on holiday in Newquay. Taking the roller for 30 yards without a board, body-surfing with the porpoises next to him. Brilliant.

The black guys were amazed. The Englishman didn't care about it being midwinter. And they'd thought the dolphins were sharks. Merv and Andy were still bashful after abandoning him in the middle of nowhere the day before. "Taught me a lesson I'll never forget," Charlie said, "Don't worry about it. I got here in the end."

They had a huge lunch in the steak house next to the hotel. Given the multi-racial nature of their group, they sat at the back of the restaurant, eating steak cooked themselves on a "hot-rock" at the table.

Charlie ate his food and thought of the orphaned twins. He'd had to raid the mini-bar to sleep the night before. Their smiles would never leave him. Their tiny mother's death would always stain his soul.

He had only one answer to such thoughts. Football. They slept for a while in their rooms after lunch, then left for the game at The Oval, right in the middle of Port Elizabeth.

A sparse crowd of around 6,000 turned up to see their relegation-threatened side fail utterly to deal with Charlie's unique talent in front of goal.

His first came after barely a minute. Quick ball out wide to Teenage, down the line to Ace, looping cross to the far-post... and Charlie came bludgeoning in to finish with his implacable forehead.

By half-time he had three and he'd let Vusi take the penalty when he'd been chopped down from behind. They trooped into the dressing-room 4-0 up… and there was "Mad-Eyes".

He was covered in a thin sheen of oil and smelt like a truck. He claimed he'd hitched a lift on a oil tanker from Durban, been discovered stowing away and thrown in the crude oil hold. Charlie wasn't sure whether to believe him or not. But as he left the dressing room with Fox's team-talk ringing in his ears ("Don't ease up Charlie, every goal could count") Dlamini said: "You have seen something English eyes have never seen before Charlie. That much I know. Learn. Remember every detail. One day you must speak the truth."

Charlie shook his head and turned his attention to the Bayi defence. They were all quite short, their determination withering after the first-half onslaught.

He wandered up to The Prof. "Everything in the air," he said, "If we need goals like Clive says, let's get goals."

The Prof's first corner was rammed home by Andy's head. The second and third went to Charlie. He dived unashamedly to win a final penalty and summoned goalkeeper Henry to score the only goal of his professional career from the spot.

Drinks were drunk in the bar that night. Charlie had scored five, they'd won 8-0 and the big Soweto clubs would have to sit up and take notice of their little cousin in KwaMashu.

They drove home via Kokstad the next morning, avoiding the border controls… and sticking to the tarmac roads.

It had been some trip. Charlie got to his room at the Edward in mid-afternoon and fell onto the bed. No training until the big game on Saturday, at home, against mid-table Jomo Cosmos.

Charlie looked at his bed-side phone. The red-light was flashing.

A message. He called reception and they put him through to an overseas number he didn't know.

It was Sarah. At the bookies in the high street back home in England. He felt a stab of homesickness just thinking about Fareham on a drizzly morning. Sarah wasn't exactly the perfect woman, but hey, they'd been together nearly a year since the first drunken snog at the Dog and Duck after beating Cambridge the season before, when he was something of a local hero.

And they'd stuck together. Until now. She was crying: "Charlie, I've done something stupid. You know Darren, the lad from the Jolly Huntsman? I done something with him. You know. Told him you'd buggered off to Africa without me. So he's only got me up the duff. Or I think it's him. Might have been you before you left…"

Charlie was reeling. "What, Darren, the left back at Gosport Borough? The fat one with tattoos and an ear-ring and a skin-head? He's a twat Sarah, you know that."

"I was lonely Charlie. I had to."

"I've only been gone bloody three weeks woman…"

"Actually Charlie, I've been seeing him for a while…"

He heard a male voice bark on the other end of the phone… either her boss at the bookies, or Darren walking in.

The line went dead.

Charlie wrestled with this latest shock in his life for some time. He tried to compartmentalize.

The football: That was good. Eight goals in three games, three wins. Very good.

The country: The beach incident with Peter, the Trojan Horse thing, Joshua, Vusi, Thulane's funeral, the resettlement camp, the orphaned twins. Awful.

The lovelife: He's scarpered when Caroline wanted him and now Sarah was pregnant by another bloke with a beer belly. Not good.

Only one solution to a set of circumstances like this, Charlie decided. Drink. Plenty of it.

The phone rings again. It's Darren, Sarah's new man. Two years ahead of him at school, a born bully, a genuine hoodlum.

"Burton, you're dead when you come home mate, Sarah says you beat her up. Gave her the fucking crabs. And now she's up the duff with a proper geezer. Come near Fareham again and I'll fucking kill you. Best stay out there with your nigger pals."

Charlie considered his response. "Darren, I never touched Sarah in my life, even when she got pissed and sold my Adidas boots last season. I haven't given her any diseases and she definitely wasn't pregnant when I left... she was on her period. So I'm in the clear mate. You're welcome to her. You should see the birds out here mate..."

"What, black girls? That's against the law there mate... you'll get arrested and put in an African jail and the big black men will bum you to death! You little shit, just you wait..."

Charlie put the phone down. His last link to home closed slowly in his head. No Sarah. No Fareham. No mum.

He drank another two mini-bottles of whisky. On a whim, he picked up the phone "international enquiries please," he said to reception. It rang, "The Evening Echo in Portsmouth, it's a newspaper," he said when a voice answered. "I'll put you through." Ringing again. "Sport please," he said. "Dunnie, it's me, Charlie Burton, the Fareham player. Listen I wanted to tell you about Africa."

Mike Dunn was the football reporter on the Portsmouth Echo, a good quality provincial daily. He's always told Charlie he was destined for greater things. "Dunnie, I got two in my first game, one in a half in my second, five last night in Port Elizabeth mate, I'm hot! You always said I had a nose for goals!"

"Brilliant news, Charlie," said Dunnie, who had spoken to Jabu on the phone as part of the scouting process, "The Chaka Royals eh? What kind of crowds you getting?"

Charlie told him everything. Dunnie, who'd left the Daily Telegraph and London a couple of years before for a quieter life in Hayling Island, scribbled it all down. "I'll get it in tomorrow Charlie, back page pal! I'll try to get some photos of you from the picture desk."

Charlie smiled. Proud. Then: "I've seen some other things Charlie. This is a bloody cruel country. I want to talk to somebody about the other shit that's going on out here."

Dunnie hesitated. "Charlie, hold that thought. Make your name banging in the goals and tell us about the other stuff when you come back. It's not safe out there."

"Okay Dunnie, good stuff, I'll call you again when I get some more goals... big game Saturday..."

"Great Charlie, speak soon..." Dunnie rang off. As Charlie put the phone down, that soft click again, like somebody else had been on the line.

By now Charlie was pleasantly pissed. The phone rang. "Is that Charlie Burton, the famous Chaka Royals goal scorer?" an extremely pleasant female voice inquired.

"Erm... yes. I think so," slurred Charlie. "Who's thish?"

"Charlie it's Caroline. I can't stop thinking about you. I go to bed every night thinking about your firm body. I've just been reading about you in the Mercury. You're a star. Even George would be proud if I got to shag the Chaka Royals top scorer!"

Charlie giggled. "We only got back this morning Caroline, sorry. I've had a few drinks. I'd better call you later."

"What room are you in Charlie?" she asked… and Charlie put the phone down, the room was circling around his head, he couldn't think about gorgeous Caroline now, not with everything else going on.

He slept. Strange dreams. Goals and death, joy and horror, football and funerals.

A knock on the door. He ignored it. More knocking. "Go away!"

Then the door opened. The chambermaid was given a note or two as Caroline gave her the master key back. The receptionist had let slip his room number. Caroline was on the prowl… and she was in his room.

Charlie had a knack of waking up quickly. Often tumescent. Caroline mistook it for real lust and acted on it. Literally.

She was vastly experienced and hungry for sex. She tore his straining boxer shorts off, took him in her mouth.

Charlie threw caution to the wind. He stripped her with an ease which surprised him. He was no great shakes in bed. Or so he thought. He just followed his instincts. He had never been with a woman like this. Lively, hungry, absolutely gorgeous. Every curve of her body was perfect, her skin was like silk… her pussy moist and magnetic. His hands found her, his tongue found her, she threw her head back, grasped his head, pulled his hair, forced him to eat her, utterly.

She screamed her climax to the entire beachfront. Then she went down on him, expertly. He writhed and stiffened. At the point of climax she stood and presented her magnificent rear, just for him. Charlie. Little Charlie with the pissed mum, the ragged clothes, the scuffed shoes.

And he took her, strong, hard delicious. Charlie felt chains fall away in his head, saw waves crashing on the shore, came like a tidal wave deep inside her from behind. Ecstasy.

It didn't end there. Caroline wouldn't allow it. They made love for two hours. Endless. She came five or six times, once twice without a break as he licked her. He fell, exhausted and sweating to the bed. And slept like a log.

When he awoke she was gone. But she'd left a note. "Great fuck!" it said, "Again. Soon. Caroline." And she'd drawn a little heart at the bottom of the page.

Bloody hell. Charlie had never known anything like it. His mind was filled with images of their two-hour tryst. He went down for dinner and kept imagining he'd glimpsed her walking across the restaurant, hips swinging, high heels clicking... demanding his body.

He couldn't sleep that night, his mind filled with images of Caroline. His initial reluctance, born of guilt and a lack of confidence, was completely swept away. He was a man utterly in love, in lust. It hadn't really happened before. Not with Judy, or Elaine... definitely not Sarah.

Had she bewitched him? Maybe "Mad Eyes" could help. He laughed at himself. And all this so soon after the horrors he had witnessed. Africa was certainly changing him, making him schizophrenic like everyone else.

He went through his normal routine in the morning. A long, long run to clear his head, then a swim. He looked for dolphins, listened for them. Nothing.

Peter pulled up a chair and chatted to him over lunch. Charlie told him all about his five goals in Port Elizabeth, then launched into the resettlement camp story. Peter was shocked, but a fuming Koos came over and put him back to work at the tables. Charlie looked up at Koos: "You ever been to a resettlement camp mate? Have you got any idea what this country is doing?"

"Englishman, you'll get yourself in the shit. And I saw the blond go up to your room yesterday. With a wedding ring. Best you shut your big mouth and go back to London."

He turned and stomped off, Charlie staring after him.

He waited for Caroline to call all afternoon. He began drinking about 5pm after another swim.

The phone finally rang at about 7. It was her. They were out somewhere. "We're at a bloody dinner party, Charlie," she said, "But I want you, I wish you were here. I want to tell all my friends about you, about my athlete, my soccer star!"

"Can I see you soon?" said Charlie, knowing he sounded too desperate, "I miss you, I need you too, my love."

It slipped out. There was a silence. "Oh, Charlie, you're so young, so innocent. Look, I'll try to come into town tomorrow night. Just be there for me. I need to be taken."

And she was gone. Charlie ached for her. All night.

He ran, swam, ate, went to the aquarium. Went out shopping and bought Caroline a necklace with Jabu's latest win bonus at a jewellers in town. He felt confident, like a new man, full of life.

His mum phoned. "Charlie, you're all over the paper!" she squealed, clearly a bit tipsy. "You're a star in Africa it says, big crowds, all the natives love you. I knew you'd make it."

"Thanks mum," said Charlie. "I'm glad I've made you proud."

"Oh, Charlie, I am." She said, "Erm… listen, I've had a few big nights since you left. I miss you so much. You couldn't send some money back could you? I'll pay you back, I promise."

Charlie spent the rest of the day waiting. There was a knock on the door at about 4pm. Caroline was in a short pink jacket, a white vesty top and a very short skirt. She looked absolutely fucking wonderful.

They didn't hesitate. They went at it like they hadn't seen each other for a decade. She came again and again, writhing, beautiful, her perfect breasts drawing him in again and again, the secret between her perfect thighs asking to be solved again and again.

It was a wonderful feeling. Powerful. Now she belonged to him. And he belonged to her.

He told Caroline that. She frowned. "Oh Charlie. So young. So fit. You could go all day couldn't you?"

He looked at her, the full length of her, presented naked on the bed. He thought his heart would burst. Every inch of her was perfect. Then a knock on the door.

Charlie leapt up. "Polisie," came the voice at the door, "Open up. You're under arrest for being an Engels doos, an English twat!"

He opened the door. Relief. It was Merv. And Andy. They'd come to say sorry for leaving him in the wilderness.

Caroline pulled the bed clothes up around her, modestly. But she'd let them see a bit of her perfect body. And she kept most of her cleavage on display as the two big footballers looked at her, hungrily.

"Fuck me," said Andy in his broad Scottish accent, "She's gorgeous!"

Merv was less approving. "Who's this," he said, "She's too old for you kid, let her have a real man."

Caroline nearly dropped her guard. The thought of taking all three of them at once appealed to her in a big way. But Charlie pushed the pair of them out the door. "Wait in the bar downstairs," he said, "We'll be down in a mo."

He went back to Caroline, kissed her long and hard, let his hands roam, grew hard again.

She pushed him away. "Come on, let's go out and party," she giggled, "With your big butch mates!"

Charlie didn't want to go. But he wanted to show off his beautiful lover to his mates. Somehow she affirmed him, made him feel complete. She was perfect, beyond his wildest dreams.

They dressed and went downstairs. Her appearance created quite a stir in the piano bar. Michelle, the faded showgirl on the piano, raised her eye-brows when Charlie appeared with the luscious blond. She liked the Englishman. This woman looked like trouble. "Charlie," she whispered while Caroline was busy flashing her eyes and cleavage at his two team-mates, "That woman's trouble."

Charlie reddened. "She's beautiful Michelle. I think I've fallen in love."

"But Charlie, look how she's dressed. That skirt's too short and if that top was any smaller it would be a handkerchief!"

Charlie frowned: "I think she looks beautiful Michelle, I can't help it."

Michelle was seriously concerned now. "Charlie, she's 15 years older than you, she's a man-eater... and she's got a bloody big engagement ring on. Oh. And a wedding band."

Charlie said: "Her husband doesn't love her anymore, she's told me. I think she'll leave him. She wants me."

"Sure she wants you Charlie, you're a handsome young bloke. But she won't leave him. He's obviously loaded. That handbag must have cost a fortune. And I bet there's kids. A huge house. She won't leave all that for sex."

Charlie blanched. "It's not just sex," but he could hear the pleading in his voice.

He turned to hear Merv telling Caroline: "You must have realised? Can't you see it? Look at his hair, his skin… Charlie's fucking half black… his dad was from Antigua or somewhere."

Charlie was about to make a joke about it, laugh it off. But Caroline froze. And gave him a long hard, top-to-toe look.

Then she turned on her heel and left the bar, bottom swinging with some gusto.

Merv looked triumphant. He'd already given the blond his number, home and work. He'd been unfaithful to his wife countless times, but never with a woman offering tits like melons and an arse like that.

The black thing was pretty conclusive. She wouldn't be back. Not for a know-nothing kid like Charlie, with no substance, no real quality. And a deep tan and black curly hair. According to the Immorality Act, one of the first Apartheid laws introduced by the Nationalists in 1958, all sexual relations between whites and non-whites were forbidden in South Africa. That act was passed a year after the banning of inter-racial marriages in the Prohibition of Mixed Marriages Act. Neither law was repealed until 1985.

Merv grinned: "Unlucky Charlie. She loves you, but she doesn't want to break the law!"

Charlie charged out of the hotel. The doorman smiled. "Have you seen a lady, pink jacket, blond hair..?"

The doorman pointed. Caroline was in deep conversation with a large white man in a safari suit. They got into a taxi together and before he could reach them, they sped off.

He never saw her again.

He didn't sleep a wink that night. He didn't want to get out of bed the next morning either.

Today they had Jomo Cosmos at the Princess Magogo. A club created by the iconic Jomo Nkomo, one of the few black South Africans to make it overseas, Cosmos had been named after the New York franchise that Nkomo had played for in the US.

They had quickly risen to challenge their older Soweto rivals and Jomo was shrewd, bringing in the best players from all over the country, black, white, brown, green, it really didn't matter.

This was a big game for the Royals. It would make or break their title charge. But Charlie was on the floor. Jabu's top-scorer was broken-hearted.

Merv came to pick him up. Charlie could barely look at his smug face, his stupid fucking moustache. He said nothing, slumped in the passenger seat. They drove to the township, he just looked at the cops as they waved them through, guns at the ready.

This was a shit country, a shit life, he wanted to go home. But to what? A shit mother, a shit ex-girlfriend, a shit Southern League future and a really shit job at the fish and chip shop?

On the corner, kids were keeping a tennis ball in the air. One, two, three, four… magical. Merv was jabbering away about Caroline and how she'd only done what's right. She had a husband and kids. He was just a fling… and a dangerously dark one at that.

Charlie watched the kids and the ball as they fell away behind them. He clutched onto the only thing he knew, the only thing that really made him happy.

Football.

Dlamini was in the dressing room. He'd been there all night. He'd had a bad feeling about the spirits. He looked at Charlie. "Your heart is cracked, Englishman. I must restore you."

He went to his cauldron, chanted some incantation, Charlie could have sworn he saw Caroline's finger with her wedding band and engagement ring, floating incongruously on the surface of his brew.

"Mad-Eyes" drew his finger across Charlie's belly. It left a line of blood. Then he smeared his foul-smelling liquid across the wound. And Charlie began to hallucinate.

He barely heard Fox's team-talk. The detailed analysis of their back four. How to keep the ball wide, watch out for their keeper, he's good on shots, weak on crosses.

Charlie was in a right state. Wobbly knees. He threw up without warning, spattering his vomit across Merv's boots. The Afrikaner jumped, spat at Charlie. It wasn't good.

It took him fully ten minutes to recognise there was actually a game going on around him. By now, the Royals were a goal down – Charlie had no idea how – and the fans were on his back. He hadn't got near the ball.

Dlamini's mad eyes were on him from the touch-line. He could feel it. The Sangoma was mouthing words to himself, playing with the small velvet bag he always drew out of some hidden recess when he was under stress.

The ball came down, out of the sky, out of the sun, like an enemy fighter in the war comics. Rather than rising to flick it on, Charlie was powerless to do anything other than let it hit him on the top of the head and he collapsed like a pack of cards. The Cosmos centre-back, a giant Sotho miner, stood on his hand, ripping the skin to the bone with his sharpened studs.

Charlie stayed down. Dlamini came on, eyes blazing. "Easy Charlie, it will come. Your heart will mend quickly this way."

He wrapped the bleeding hand in some sort of poultice. It smelt of chicken and blood. Shit, it hurt like buggery.

But as he stood, he realized the dizziness had receded. He couldn't remember much about the last twenty minutes but he was suddenly focused on events going on around him. The fans booing, the Cosmos players sniggering. In his heart, he was angry. No longer self-pitying, submissive.

The Prof was on the free-kick, which the referee had inexplicably given for Charlie being hit on the head by the ball. Charlie wandered to his right. The Prof took the big run-up… but instead of shooting, he laid it to Charlie.

The big defender came charging in, expecting another comfortable challenge. Like taking candy from a baby.

As he came, Charlie flicked the ball over his head, jinked around the onrushing giant, and lashed a shot with a ferocity he had rarely felt before.

It bent like a banana, flew like a tracer bullet… the keeper, a highly-paid Paraguayan, was flummoxed. And the ball thudded against the angle between post and bar. Drat.

Charlie's head – and heart – were in the right place now though. Three times he took the ball with his back to goal, executed a series of near-perfect Cruyff turns and roared past his cumbersome markers to make chances for his invigorated team-mates.

Then, again in the "psychologically crucial" period just before the break, he felt the need to go wide right, out of the centre-forward's "corridor of doom". It was as if his boots were dragging him out. Ace looked at him quizzically and, without a word exchanged between them, he drifted into the centre, taking up Charlie's position.

Vusi had the ball at full-back. He beat his man and pushed it up the line to Charlie down the right wing. Charlie controlled on the run, beat the incoming midfielder on the run, produced a ridiculous turn-in-flight to lose the next marker, then a couple of step-overs and he was clear, breaking into open space behind the defence.

He looked up. Teenage, neglected and quiet since Charlie's arrival, was wandering aimlessly forward on the far post. Charlie yelled: "Near post, Teenage!"

And the lightweight striker began to move, pace quickening. Charlie cut in, beat the centre-half then produced a delightful chip. Teenage couldn't miss. The ball sat up in front of his forehead and the little man, too Christian to complain about his lot as the butt of most jokes, simply poked his head at the ball, stuck it in the corner, and happily registered the first headed goal of his long professional career. Magnificent.

Charlie celebrated with the rest of them, with wild, unrestrained glee.

Jomo Nkomo, heavy but well-balanced, was warming himself up on the side. One of the black population's great icons after his time in the States, he had even opened the first Kentucky Fried Chicken outlets in the Soweto sprawl.

A businessman, millionaire and pin-up, Nkomo could still play football.

After a roasting from Fox at half-time, the Royals emerged to find the great man changed and ready. Like Kaizer Molefe, the founder of the legendary Chiefs, Jono had made his name the hard way. Up through the ranks of Sowetan football and on to the big time in a world not eager to welcome black footballers plying their trade overseas.

If he could get a passport and travel freely around the world under Apartheid, Charlie suspected Nkomo, now deep into his 30s, could certainly work out how to destroy the Royals defence.

He did. Swiftly. Nkomo and Roy Wegerle, one of the few white players readily accepted in the townships, weaved their magic. Wegerle, later to move for millions around the mid-ranking English clubs like QPR and Blackburn, would go on to play for the United States in the World Cup finals as an experienced professional.

But for now, he was a young, hungry winger. While all the focus was on Nkomo, Wegerle was making the play. Charlie realised it too late. He cut down the right, just as Charlie had, and found his manager and owner arriving late in the area. Wegerle located him with a neat cut-back ball and Nkomo flicked it beyond a flailing McGeechan and rammed the ball into the corner past a hopeless Henry. Shit. 2-1 down.

Wegerle was at it again almost from the kick-off, playing a swift one-two with Nkomo, then breaking through on goal past a square defence. As he raised his foot to shoot, he was surprised to see a English boot snake out in front of him and, instead of just sliding the ball out of play, Charlie – who had made fifty yards when he saw the break – hooked the ball back with his heel. Wegerle went flying over his out-stretched leg. Charlie stood up, the ball at his feet, like a triumphant gladiator.

In the far distance, The Prof was already on the move. Charlie took three paces with the ball, and as the Cosmos converged on him, he hit a ball with the outside of his right foot which cut the Cosmos defence in two. The Prof took the ball down elegantly, squiggled an artistic dash through two defenders, and lobbed the Paraguayan keeper as he came out to narrow the angle. It was 2-2. Some game.

Nkomo hit the post with a free-kick as he tried desperately to break the deadlock. Then a Merv throw-in was flicked on by Teenage, suddenly realising the importance of having a footballing head on his shoulders, but though it looped over the keeper, there was a defender to clear off the line.

And so to the final seconds of an enthralling encounter. The Prof – who else? – opened up space on the halfway line. Moses Faya, back from injury and off the bench, broke down the right. The defender flew in, brought him down, but Faya recovered, put in a bobbling low cross. The defender sliced his clearance high in the air. It was dropping on the edge of the arc, about 22 yards out. Charlie let the ball fall over his shoulder, about to attempt one of the most difficult volleys in football. He pulled it off with aplomb. This new feeling, this instinct he appeared to have developed under Dlamini's mad eye, kicked in. He struck the ball as it dropped, his shape perfect to meet it. A rocket. If the Paraguayan had got behind it, he might have ended up back in the Andes. It nearly broke the net, it certainly broke Cosmos hearts. What a goal, what a game. The Royals 3-2 and, for a few hours at least, top of the table. Incredible.

The whistle went before Cosmos could kick off. Nkomo mastered his fury and approached Charlie: "Fucking brilliant mate. Great game. I'll give you anything you want. Sign for me. Tonight."

Charlie grinned: "And let Jabu down? Sorry Mr Nkomo, I can't do that. But thanks for the game. You can certainly play a bit!"

Nkomo smiled and patted his belly. "Not for much longer," he smiled, "One day this country is going to play in the World Cup and I'll be too old. But I'll be the boss, and I don't mind picking coloureds."

"Sorry, Mr Nkomo, I'm English… but I think my dad was from Jamaica…"

Wegerle came up. "Great tackle, Charlie, thought I had you there. You English? Know anyone over there wants a right wing?"

Charlie grinned. The afternoon was a joy. The Cosmos players, black, white and in between, came back to the shebeen for drinks. Plenty of them. Nkomo was a giant of a man in all ways. Wegerle, apart from being a brilliant footballer, was a high-jump champion, first class cricketer and basketballer. It was the kind of day every footballer loves. Great game, great post-game. And Charlie had taken his tally to ten from four games. Not bad!

Jabu wandered over as Charlie spoke to Wegerle and Nkomo. "You're not signing for them Charlie, I'll get "Mad-Eyes" to put a spell on you if you do!"

Nkomo laughed: "You think I haven't tried? Too loyal this Englishman! And his heart's in the right place Jabu, look after him. Get him over here. One day this nation will need footballers like him and Roy – and Teenage. I didn't know he could head the bloody ball!"

Charlie's concentration on the conversation between these two township greats was interrupted by a presence. Not for the first time he spotted the girl. It was Sophie. Charlie had seen her in Jabu's office a couple of times. She was a secretary, but more than that. A personal assistant, is that what you called it these days?

She was the one who battled with the Department of Bantu Affairs to keep the players legal, with stamped bona fide Pass Books. She was the one who persuaded Holiday Inns and South African Airways to take their multi-racial bookings. She made sure everyone was paid, that the tax man was vaguely happy with the way the club ran. And she dealt with the Zulu Royal family and the leaders of their political arm, Inkatha, when they wanted tickets or publicity with The Prof or Ace.

Charlie had noticed her. Of course he had. She was beautiful. But in the office, she wore a suit. Severe, unfussy.

Here in the shebeen she was like a walking beam of African sunlight. Charlie couldn't take his eyes of her as she walked across the room, networking with footballers, local taxi drivers, hoodlums and tramps. She treated them all the same: beaming smile, reassuring hand-shake, gentle words… but firm.

Jabu caught him. "Sophie's off-limits Englishman. She's my cousin! The world is chasing that woman and she doesn't notice!"

Charlie went bright red, embarrassed. "My heart's broken anyway Jabu. Some bloody blond in town. Merv told her I was black and illegal… and she buggered off!"

"I heard," said Jabu, chewing his lip. "Look, I know it's hard. You're lonely, you're in a strange country. As a special present for your ninth goal, how about I ask Sophie to drive you home tonight, make sure you're okay? She won't sleep with you, but she'll make you feel better."

Mad-Eyes appeared, as he always did, out of nowhere. "This is as it should be, Charlie. The blond women broke your heart with devil's magic. Sophie is an angel. She will fix you good. But go easy. Know she is not from London. You are not from KwaMashu. And soon you will need cattle."

The last remark threw Charlie a bit, but Dlamini was always coming out with strange stuff. You never understood until it was too late with Mad-Eyes. Charlie smiled. He had expected to feel devastated tonight, no matter what happened at football.

But somehow, his heart was strong. And Sophie was talking to Jabu. She smiled her bright smile as he whispered. She responded easily to his request, if anything her eyes sparkled still more.

She came over. "Charles Ivor Burton, you've already had too much to drink," she said, firm but fair, "Say goodbye to your friends, get your scoring boots, and I'll drive you back to the Edward. I need to speak to the receptionist about your phone bill anyway, you naughty boy!"

It was just what Charlie needed. A good talking to. He shot over to the Cosmos lads, shook their hands warmly, with a variety of African handshakes. He went to Vusi, hugged him. "Every goal is for Thulane," he said, "Every point is for all of us."

Vusi smiled. It was rare these days. The Prof stood and hugged him. Dlamini glared, which was probably the best Charlie could expect from him. Charlie whispered: "I know what you've done for me, Mad-Eyes. I thank you for it. I hope one day I can repay you."

Dlamini, who had not heard his conversation with Vusi, said: "Every goal is for us, every point is for all of us. We are a people deprived of our rights. Football is all we have. Use your talents Charlie. I will help you."

Nkomo jokingly got his cheque book out and waved it at him in front of Jabu, Wegerle handed him a card with a telephone number on, the Paraguayan keeper simply frowned.

Charlie and Sophie were away. Into her nippy Nissan Cherry. Most black people walked miles to work, many took crowded trains, others piled onto badly-maintained buses. Sophie was one of the few with her own transport. And her car was newer than any in the townships, hardly rusty at all. Untouched by the Tsotsis too.

Charlie sat back in the passenger seat. His boots clasped defensively in his lap. She smiled: "I'm not going to bite you Charlie. Jabu has just told me to drive you home and check you are okay. He says some woman tried to steal your heart. You are lonely, you are a long way from home, you need a strong heart to win the double for the Royals. So this is just part of the service!"

Charlie realised Sophie had always been special. He tried to compare her to Caroline, all tits and arse, legs and lipstick.

Thing is, how many black women were presented as sex-symbols? Sophie had full breasts, child-bearing hips. How many beautiful black people had he ever considered beautiful? Shirley Bassey? Was that it?

And what had the chambermaid said to him the other day when he paid her a compliment. "I'm not big enough," she'd sad, sadly, "My people value big women, the kind who can have plenty of children. We don't want to grow old alone on a pension, we want to be surrounded by children. But the magazines are all about skin-lighteners, hair straighteners and diets. We are a lost generation."

But Sophie wasn't lost. She was confident in her beauty. Her hair was proudly African, filled with decoration tonight in the Shebeen. She had a low-cut top, not the stiff white shirt from the office. And a cleavage to die for, perfect breasts. And her legs were good, strong legs. God she was beautiful he thought, looking sideways at Jabu's cousin.

"You know The Professor is my father?" she grinned. "Mlungisi is Jabu's half-brother. Their father was an induna with many wives. We are all family at the Royals!"

"What?" said Charlie, "How can that be? How old are you? How old is The Prof?"

"He's nearly 40," she smiled, "I was born when he was 17. I'm 22. And you?"

She looked at Charlie. Shy, quiet... but magnificent on the football field. And with a heart of gold, judging by his actions and words so far. He was genuinely infuriated by the rampant racism he saw all around him.

Jabu had no idea, but she'd spoken to everyone about this strange, dark-skinned Englishman who had lit up their lives in the last three weeks. And few had a bad word to say about him.

She'd spoken to his mother, and felt only sympathy. She'd found Peter at the hotel, given him some money for his pain at the hands of the police . And he had been glowing about Charlie. Even Vusi, the arch-revolutionary, liked the boy.

"I'm 23, Sophie," he said quietly, "And I've never really been happy. Can you help me? I feel like my life is changing here, but I took a wrong turn with this Caroline woman. And I keep getting into trouble, seeing terrible things. It gets to me, deep down. The resettlement camp, the shootings, the funeral. It's terrible. But this country is beautiful, your people have been so good to me."

Sophie smiled inside and out. "Not many Englishmen would have seen through it all like you Charlie. And still scored goals! How about we be friends. We can explore the world together, here in South Africa and maybe, one day, over the seas."

Then, as always, the sirens. A police car had seen them at the traffic lights as they began to enter central Durban. Sophie looked anxiously in her rear-view mirror. She rarely ventured into the city at night. Blacks in their own cars were likely to be harassed by the police after dark. There was a curfew against her people in the suburbs and the city centres when night fell.

Charlie frowned. The police car was hot on their trail. Sirens sounding, one of the cops leaned out of a window with a revolver in his hand.

"Drive, Sophie!" he said, "They think we're breaking the law... they're going to shoot."

Sophie put her foot down. The little Nissan shot forward... and two gun shots rang out.

The back windscreen shattered, Sophie screamed. The back tyre went with a bang. The car swerved and rolled. And rolled. Chaos. Darkness.

CHAPTER 6: IMMORTALITY

"When an enemy digs a grave for you, God gives you an emergency exit "
                              Kirundi Proverb (Burundi)

Charlie came to in a panic. He could smell petrol. Sophie was sobbing next to him. They were upside down. Charlie could see a bullet-hole punched clean through his head-rest. It must have missed narrowly, or bounced off his thick head. His anger at what the police had done took over. "It's okay Sophie, I'll get you out."

"My leg Charlie, my leg. It's trapped. Please..."

Charlie slipped out of his seat-belt. His window was shattered, he kicked the glass out and slid into the open air from under the car. Two policemen rushed forward, guns drawn. Charlie looked at them, they screamed, but he walked around the front of the car, got to Sophie's side and, with a strength which came from somewhere deep inside him, he lifted the car. He strained and heaved. The two coppers put their guns away and joined in. The car, with the engine still running, reluctantly righted itself, slamming back down on four mangled wheels.

Charlie grunted, pulled at the driver's door frame. It came open with a bang, Charlie went flying. He was up. He hugged Sophie. "It's okay, it's okay," he re-assured her.

Flames began to flicker from the bonnet. The policemen began to edge away. Charlie crouched down into the chairwell. Her foot was trapped by bent metal. Heat was coming through from the engine. Petrol was soaking into the carpet. Calm, he pushed the seat back as far as it would go. "Pull that leg Sophie, pull. Or we both die."

She pulled, screaming, crying. He was crouched in front of her, his back now wedged under the distorted dashboard. More superhuman effort, and suddenly everything shifted with a wrench. Her foot came free. She sobbed. Charlie fell forward on to her, caught her by her midriff, smelling her perfume, the essence of a distraught Sophie, and lifted her out of the car and away.

He had walked about ten yards when the car burst into flames. No real explosion, just a "whump" as the whole thing caught light. The heat was incredible, the flames nearly invisible. Ten more seconds…

Charlie put Sophie down gently. Ever so gently. He looked at the two policemen. They drew their guns and smiled anxiously. "Nou luister, now listen, you were driving with a black woman at night, what do you expect us to do? You should have pulled over…"

Charlie's temper held. Barely. He looked at them and stood up to his full height, just short of six foot. They were both a couple of inches shorter.

"I'll tell you what we're going to do." He said quietly, menacingly. "I'm not going to tell the British Consulate that you two shot at an unarmed member of their diplomatic service. You two are going to drive me back to the Edward Hotel where I am a well-known face. And then you are going to leave us to sort all this mess out. If I ever see either of you again, I'll get MI5 involved. You ever seen a James Bond film?"

The two coppers, young and inexperienced, cowered in front of his controlled wrath. Then they walked to the car. Charlie opened the door for Sophie, helped her in. Her foot was bleeding. The policemen drove them to the Edward and, obediently, dropped them off outside the hotel.

One of them got out., "Listen, Englishman, you can't drive around the city at night with a black woman. It's not done. I'm sorry. We shouldn't have fired. Things are very tense around here. Everyone's got guns. Blacks, whites, Indians. It's shoot first or be shot."

"Then your nation will burn," said Charlie. "If you fire five bullets at people for driving into town at night, nobody is safe. And you're supposed to be here to keep the place peaceful. Go... forget all this. But next time you see a situation, for Christ's sake think before you shoot. Please."

The copper in the car shouted something in Afrikaans. His mate edged away. Charlie turned, and helped Sophie up as she sat in obvious pain on the steps of the hotel.

They went around the back of the Edward, the Bantu entrance. Peter was there, cleaning his shoes. He looked up: "Englishman, are you okay?" He helped them up to his room. Charlie called the hospital in Overport. Asked for Piet Vermeulen, the doctor who had treated Joshua.

Mercifully, he answered. There was something to be said for 72-hour shifts. Piet listened. "They won't leave it Charlie. They'll come for you. You might have intimidated two coppers, but BOSS will hear of this. Time to move hotels. I'll be there in ten minutes."

Remarkably, he was. In a white estate with a red cross on it. He drove them up into the Berea, the plush white suburb above Durban. "You'll be safe here," he said, "The police and other people were asking about you at the hospital. They're closing in on you. They know you saw the Trojan Horse thing. Come on."

He took them into a plush house with a small square swimming pool in a quadrangle in the middle. It was beautifully decorated, pure opulence. "Mum and dad's place," Piet said, "Now let me look at that foot."

He dealt expertly with Sophie's crushed right foot. Given they'd had five bullets fired through the back windscreen and rolled three times at 60 mph, they had got off lightly.

Charlie phoned Jabu, told him everything. Then he gave the phone to Sophie, who spoke quickly but calmly while Piet finished bandaging her wounds.

Then Piet got up. "Now you, Charlie. Look in the mirror."

Charlie looked over his shoulder at a full-length rear-view of himself. He'd been hit in the right buttock. Blood down his green tracksuit. Piet pulled Charlie's trousers down, unabashed. "Just creased by a bullet mate, you were lucky. Couple of stitches should do it."

The adrenaline of the crash was wearing off. Charlie yelped as the needle passed in and out. He put butterfly stitches on a nasty gash over Charlie's left eyebrow. He hadn't felt that one either. And Piet peered at Charlie's left ear. "Something here. A bullet I think. Just took a nip out of your ear. How lucky is that!"

Jabu turned up in the morning, early. Before the white businessmen had woken, his workers had got hold of the burnt-out Nissan and whisked it off to the sugar cane fields. A new Nissan with identical number plates had appeared magically outside the house. Jabu and The Prof spoke for a long time to Sophie. Then they turned to him. "You did well Englishman. They won't find you here. But they'll ask questions when they find you. Deny everything. Tell them you are going home soon. Sophie will drive you to football from now on. Merv can't be trusted. Don't tell anybody where you're living. I need a few more goals, a few more games. Then you can go tell the truth about paradise."

There was no training that night. Sophie went to work as normal. The police turned up at the Royals offices and questioned her. Jabu had a high-powered white lawyer in the office, just by chance. He soon saw them off. They looked at her spotless Nissan and left, shrugging.

Piet woke up and re-dressed Charlie's wounds. Sophie and Jabu came round. Surprisingly, Piet could talk some Zulu. He politely declined the bundle of notes Jabu tried to give him.

"Jabu, let me come train with you tonight, man. I played for Wits. I can play for you. I'm sick of just going from the hospital to home every night. I need to get out more. Let me come see KwaMashu!"

Jabu liked the idea. Piet in his military doctor's uniform would ease Charlie's passage to training, no question.

The rest of the week passed in relative peace. Charlie ran the streets of the Berea every day, pushing himself up the steep hillside, relieved to find the wounds from the police incident hadn't left a lasting legacy. Just a pain in the bum and a lump out of his ear. Then he returned and worked on Piet's sophisticated weights room. Then a swim, a late lunch.

Piet and Sophie would come home, they'd eat together, and Piet and Charlie went off to training.

Piet was about 6ft 2in, skinny as a rake. He had a good engine, could run forever… and Fox agreed to let him train with the rest of the team after ten minutes of five-a-side.

Interestingly, it was Merv who complained about "another white guy", not the rest of the team.

By the end of the week, Jabu and Sophie had sorted his paperwork and Piet was eligible to play for the Royals.

But it was after training Charlie really enjoyed. The three of them, Sophie, Piet and Charlie, would talk and talk.

Piet was a bright bloke, a liberal South African, like so many of the rich, English-speaking types from Joburg. And he knew his stuff; politics, religion, popular culture, history, communism, capitalism.

Sophie matched him argument for argument. Piet wanted a more democratic South Africa with a return to the "qualified franchise" some blacks and coloureds had enjoyed under English rule and the United Party, before the Nationalists came to power in '48. "Let the rich blacks vote, no problem," said Piet, "We need a black middle class. It's the only way this country can gradually become normal. Make it a class divide, not race. But tell the Afrikaners you're handing out one man, one vote, and it's one white, one boat.

"Seriously, most of the older Afrikaners are working class, uneducated. They need Apartheid to give them status. Their white skin is all they have to keep them from being beggars and lowly labourers. Threaten that and they'll bring out the sjamboks and the guns."

Sophie was having none of it; "Qualified franchise? When blacks can't even get proper jobs? You'll end up with a couple of thousand blacks living like whites and the majority will still want their freedom. It won't stop the riots, the demonstrations, the bombings. It's all or nothing. Release the Rivonia prisoners. Give Mandela a chance to lead the revolution and it will be bloodless. You'll see."

Charlie felt out of his depth. And utterly bewitched by Sophie. By the weekend, he had the chance to do his talking. With his football boots.

But this was no ordinary game. Orlando Pirates, one of South Africa's biggest sides, lay in wait. Sophie and Jabu had managed to get papers for the whole team to take a flight to Joburg from Durban airport. The team were excited, restless as they waited in the departure lounge. Vusi had never flown before.

Piet talked him through it. Dressed in his army uniform. Charlie had opened Vusi's eyes, Piet opened them still further. Here was a guy, white and working within the system, who was bending it from the inside. He had gone public with his complaints about the routine sterilisation of black female patients at the hospital. He had refused to turn over Joshua to BOSS. Vusi knew this. Couldn't understand why a white South African was on his side. Like many Zulus, he almost preferred the overt racism of the Afrikaner to the soft-soap of the English liberals. But this guy could play football too. He was on the bench for tomorrow's game, ready to come on and shore up the midfield against some of the best players in Africa.

Charlie giggled. Piet was holding Vusi's hand as they took off, reassuring him. Sophie was busily ensuring The Prof didn't get on the free drinks. Her father had spent his best years looking into a bottle, only her close attention had dragged him out of alcoholism and back onto the football field.

The rest of the team congregated around Charlie, asking him questions about Spain and Greece and other places he had seen, other airplanes he had flown in.

Jabu smiled. Dlamini wouldn't fly. He'd left days before, making his way to Johannnesburg by train... or car... or horse. He'd get there somehow. Might even be in the dressing room now, with his shovel of Princess Magogo soil, his cauldron and his velvet bag.

And look at my team, he thought, getting on at last. Sure, Merv was still on the outside, but he had that long throw.

Andy was adapting fast since Charlie's arrival. And Piet, according to Clive Fox, was a fair player. He'd checked with the coaches at Wits, they recommended him. Though apparently he was an even better cricketer. Stupid game.

Jabu had never travelled to "The Buccaneers" with much confidence before. The ref would always be against them, the crowd would be massive and intimidating, they would pay their players more than Jabu could ever hope to afford.

But today, as they headed to the Holiday Inns near the airport,

Jabu felt he was on the verge of something positive, something good. And Charlie was at the centre of it. Charlie and Sophie, who hadn't stopped looking at the Englishman since boarding.

Fox gave a rousing speech in the restaurant when they got to the hotel. They ate and bonded. Charlie roomed with The Prof, Piet with Vusi. Jabu and Clive liked that. "I've never enjoyed my job so much, Jabu," Clive said, "It's like we're a team at last. Black and white. We just need to sign some purples and greens."

Clive was a pragmatic bloke. Barely 5ft 6in, he'd been a good but not great right back at Durban City. He'd tried to get them to the top of the game under the new National Professional League, but the fans had drifted away, frightened by the blacks flooding to their games.

Durban City had won the title twice and Fox had seen the future in the townships. But he hadn't much enjoyed it. Until now. Suddenly he could compete at the top level, they had a massive fan base and interest from the white journalist was growing fast. Perhaps, one day, white people would come to watch football again.

They travelled to Soweto in a luxury bus, organised by Laura, Piet's girlfriend, who lived in Sandton, just outside Joburg. She was gorgeous, friendly, entirely at home among the Zulus but clearly not comfortable with Merv and his wandering hands.

Piet laughed: "Laura can look after herself. She's going to enjoy today more than anyone."

Everywhere they looked, people on the side of the road were making Pirates signs at the Royals bus, the hands overlapping above their heads in the skull-and-crossbones of the Buccaneers' flag.

When they got to the Orlando Stadium in the middle of Soweto, the place was mobbed. Pirates were the more working class option for the local populace. They were the team of the people. One of the black institutions which had survived and thrived through the sick years of Apartheid.

But today there would be no room for sentiment. The Royals were the team of their people, the proud Zulu. And about 500 of them had managed to get to the game, where they joined around the same number from the local mining hostels, where they worked as migrant labour.

The Royals stood huddled in the centre circle while most of the 40,000 crowd booed and whistled at the visitors. Charlie and Piet watched amazed as insane Royals fans snuck around the back of the huge bowl, then tore through the Pirates fans. This maddened the home support, who grabbed at their clothes, lashed out with sticks and weapons. But still the single Zulu fans ploughed on down the stands, until they emerged at the front, clambered quickly over the 12 foot perimeter fence, where they were arrested, roughly, by the stewards. But not before, blood-soaked and naked, they had taken the applause of the whole stadium for their pointless courage.

Inspired by such madness, Dlamini appeared. He went around whispering strange things in various ears. Stopped next to Piet. And pulled out a stethoscope. He put it on Piet's chest. The whole team stared. Then he pulled back, put a thoughtful finger to his lips and said: "Your heart is good, Piet Vermeulen. Very good for a Boer!"

They laughed at that, then went quiet as Dlamini went about his work in the dressing room. Dlamini looked at Charlie's bullet wounds, tutted, and moved on. Piet took the messy ribbon around his midriff without a fuss. He was only a substitute, but everyone got the treatment from "Mad Eyes", and everyone had to walk through the sludge of urine and mud at the dressing room door.

Jabu had been told the referee would be George Thebe. But clearly his performance at their last game wasn't good enough for the Pirates. They had brought in Ranjith Naidoo, a tall, Indian official, proud and unbendable. Well, nearly.

The Pirates were a mean side, strong at the back, talented up front but not prolific. The first-half was an ugly thing of few chances. Charlie had one snap shot from the edge of the box, under pressure. He struck it sweetly as he was cut down from behind... but his shot cannoned off the bar.

Fox brought on Piet for the second half, shifting things around and bringing off a clearly unhappy Merv. Dlamini was looking anxious until that point. As Piet left the dressing room, ready for his second-half debut, the mad medicine man neatly snipped a tuft of hair from the back of Piet's head and snuck it in his velvet bag. Charlie noticed, a confident smile passed between the two men.

Pirates struck early in the second half, a superb goal from their well-muscled centre-forward Philemon Masinga, who would go on to play for Leeds United. But Charlie wasn't worried. They were running out of steam in the midfield and Coach Clive had pushed Piet on into the middle of the park, where he was winning more and more of the ball and freeing up The Prof and Faya to attack the pressurized Pirates.

The home team's Chilean manager was struggling to make himself understood, pushing his defence up and demanding a stream of questionable off-side decisions from referee Naidoo. It worked up to a point.

Until The Prof took a neat, short ball from Piet and dinked it over the top. Charlie was moving long before the ball was played. By the time the defence turned, he was clear. The linesman, clearly one-eyed, raised his flag but Naidoo ignored him. Charlie had been at least a yard onside.

The Orlando Stadium wasn't the best of surfaces but Charlie let the ball run in front of him. Their keeper, a big white guy, came out to narrow the angle. Charlie shaped to shoot, the keeper made himself big... and fell for the dummy. Charlie pushed the ball to the right, the keeper dived in vain, and Charlie was left to roll the equaliser into an empty net.

Ten minutes from time, with the Pirates pushing but puffing, Vusi unleashed a long clearance. Perfect. Teenage, still firmly believing he was now a major force in the air, went up for the flick-on and Charlie gambled. The ball came off the back of the defenders head and he was through again. The keeper came, expecting a dummy. He didn't get one. Charlie simply hit the ball from fully 35 yards as it bounced up nicely in front of him. He caught it just right, dipping onto the underside of the bar, where it bounced down and over the line. Faya followed up and stuck the ball away, but it was unnecessary, everyone in the stadium knew Charlie had scored. The linesman flagged again, Naidoo went to talk to him... and gave the goal.

Charlie, celebrating, suddenly noticed the far end, the real fanatical Pirates end, was emptying fast. Going home already? Then, frighteningly, thousands of fans came storming over the far fence. The weight of them bent the supports and, after an agonizing few seconds, the whole thing fell. Hundreds came storming onto the field. Dozens were left crushed under the weight of the falling fence, their shoes stuck in the mesh.

They caught the referee near the tunnel, kicking him, beating him. Charlie could see stewards – there were no police – hitting at the fans with sjamboks and even a huge metal panga. But they were a mob now. Nobody was going to stop them. Charlie was stunned. All he could see was the referee's black socks and boots sticking out from the melee as he was beaten.

Piet didn't hesitate. He grabbed a foot, shouted: "Help me!" and Charlie joined him. The pair of them dragged Ranjith Naidoo away. The mob turned, no individuals, just an angry monster, hungry for blood. And a gun-shot went off. It was Merv. Substituted at half-time, he'd gone off in a sulk and had a shower. And put his jacket on. With his favourite Glock in the pocket "because anything could happen in Soweto".

He fired two shots in the air. The mob stalled. Charlie and Piet picked up the ref and bundled him into the tunnel. The rest of the team were right behind them, shouting, fighting the angry fans. Merv stood in the tunnel, and fired into the roof. The bullet ricocheted off the concrete, alarmingly.

But the fans came to a stop again. The Royals locked themselves in their dressing room. "What about Laura and Sophie?" said Charlie. Piet blanched. The Prof calmed them: "Jabu is with them, he'll look after them."

Merv banged on the door from the outside. They'd locked him out. Vusi opened the door reluctantly. Merv came in, sweating. "Saved you all," he sneered, and went and threw up in the toilets.

The game had been live on SABC2 the "Bantu" television channel. The nation knew what had happened. Sirens began to sound, they could hear a helicopter. If one place could be guaranteed a quick police response to a riot, it was Soweto since '76.

The referee wasn't in bad shape, considering the kicking he'd taken. He sat up, Piet treated him, gave him water. Felt his bruised arm and ribs. "You've broken a couple of those Ranjith," he said, "But nothing life-threatening to worry about. Guess we all got lucky."

The siege mentality gradually dissipated in the claustrophobic dressing room. They could hear the shouts of the police in Afrikaans. A knock on the door. Jabu with the girls and other officials.

Charlie hugged Sophie, Piet took Laura in his arms. An ambulance crew put Ranjith on a stretcher, and whisked him away. But now there were gunshots and screams echoing down the tunnel.

Charlie emerged onto the field where he had scored two more memorable goals – and witnessed the carnage as the police tore into anyone they could see. The helicopter overhead was guiding them in and spraying tear-gas indiscriminately at anyone and everything.

The drum majorettes in their smart uniforms were getting it too. They sat huddled in a corner, beyond the broken fence, crying while the police berated them, taunted them. Charlie ran over. "For fuck's sake guys, these girls aren't the trouble makers. Let them be."

The Prof was beside him. Together they shepherded the schoolgirls out of the stadium to their bus. All around them, policemen were laying into fans with sjamboks and night sticks. And more gunfire.

Charlie felt sick inside. The luxury bus had been stoned by fans, then shot up by the police. They returned quietly to the hotel in taxis. The flight home was not quite the celebration it should have been.

Next day, the newspapers and the news bulletins made a big deal of the riot. Ref Naidoo was interviewed, as was the local police commissioner, who talked darkly about "uncontrollable masses" who attended football games.

No mention was made of the result, confirmed later in the day as a final score despite the abandonment of the game, as a 2-1 win which lifted the Royals back to the top of the table.

Charlie read it all. And realised Naidoo, the ref, was from Chatsworth, an Indian area in Durban. And that he would soon be transferred to the Addington Hospital in the city centre to be nearer his family.

Tuesday morning he took a long run. Down into the city, through the busy streets, until he got to the hospital. There weren't many Indian names on the sister's sheet.

He soon found Naidoo, who smiled as he entered the room. "Charlie Burton," he grinned, "I made sure you got the credit for both goals!"

Charlie sat with him, gave him the grapes he'd purchased from a street vendor outside."What was that all about Ranjith, why did that happen?"

Naidoo shrugged: "They offered me a bribe, I turned it down. They thought because I was an Indian from Durban I would be biased against the Zulus after Cato Manor…"

"Cato Manor…?"

"A riot, when they were trying to implement the Urban Areas act. Cato Manor was a black and Indian area. The Government wanted it cleared. Riots broke out. The Zulus attacked the Indians, like they always do. Even in Uganda and Kenya, we are still foreigners in Africa, even after generations on these shores."

Charlie leapt to an immediate conclusion: "So the Indians are kind of an in-between layer here. You'd side with the whites if the crunch came wouldn't you?"

Naidoo wasn't so sure: "Maybe. We're certainly better off than the blacks. The government want us to have our own political parties, us and the coloureds. I suppose eventually they'll try to make an alliance between whites, coloureds and Indians, as long as the National Party is in charge. That way, they'll have about seven million "non-blacks" and about 22 million blacks. Just have to make more homelands!

"But the young guys in our community don't see it that way. They see us as black, not half-black. The bright young guys at the universities want us to join in with the ANC and fight the Nationalists. Make sure we are seen as part of the solution, not part of the problem, so there isn't a Uganda-style conclusion, when Idi Amin threw all the Asians out in 1972 after he took control.

"Indians are an important part of South Africa. Ghandi grew up here. He was thrown off a train, that's what started him off. There are millions of us, we have money, businesses… and we don't want to go back to India and Pakistan, we don't belong there. But what will happen to us, I don't know. The whites don't want us, the blacks don't trust us."

Charlie's head ached. He hadn't thought about all the graduations between black and white. Way he saw it, everyone was pretty much the same. There should be laws against people who create divisions, classify people as black… just because their dad was from the Ivory Coast or whatever.

Then a young white nurse came in with the sister. "Ugh," she said, "I'm not dealing with a coolie."

Charlie stood, angry, but Ranjith's family were arriving. "You can take him home," said the sister, "We can't treat broken ribs."

Charlie shook his head, shook their hands. And left in confusion.

CHAPTER 7: LOSING

"One who bathes willingly with cold water doesn't feel the cold."

Fipa Proverb (Tanzania)

Charlie left the hospital at a trot. He weaved through the busy streets, up towards the market. Strangely, in the middle of the city, the well-heeled white population look miserable and spoke little. Up by the market, the dirt-poor seemed happier, louder, more colourful.

But after a mile or so, he became aware of a car just over his shoulder. Travelling slowly, at his pace. He stopped to do up his laces. He glanced at the car out of the corner of his eye. The Inspektor was driving, in dark glasses. Talking into a walkie-talkie. Charlie stood and upped the pace. As he ran through the main streets of Durban, he spotted a long sign along the wide of the building. NATAL MERCURY it said. He ran straight in. They had a metal detector on the door. A couple of years before a bomb had gone off at the nearby Rivonia Hotel. Later an attempted coup in the Seychelles had been organized there. The son of the famous mercenary Mike Hoare worked as a sub-editor at the Mercury. Security was tight. But they let Charlie in after a quick call to Solomon, the photographer, upstairs.

Solomon greeted him warmly on the second floor. They wandered through the busy corridors, Charlie telling Solomon about the riot, how they had got Ranjith out, how Merv's gun had kept the mob at bay. He told about the police afterwards… and his visit to the hospital. He didn't mention he'd been followed here by BOSS. Mere detail!

Solomon went to a terminal and began to write. The two old white guys, Fred and Dennis frowned. Solomon was a photographer, not a writer. And he was black. Charlie helped him. They wrote it together, Charlie remembering details and adding quotes. It was a good piece and ran the next day under the headline: "Cheerful Charlie undaunted by Pirate attack."

The editor loved it. So did the boss of the Zulu paper, Ilanga, who offered Solomon a writer's job on the spot.

Charlie picked up a phone."How do I get an outside line," he asked Solomon. "Dial Zero" he said, curious.

Charlie called Dunnie in Portsmouth. He talked him through the latest chapter of his African adventure. And told him about BOSS following him. And the twins in the resettlement camp who haunted his dreams.

Dunnie, distantly, felt for young Charlie. He would write about the local lad who had scored nine goals in four games at the top level in South Africa. The rest was beyond him.

"Charlie, I've recorded this call," he said, "I'm going to play this tape to Neil Harris, the Daily Mail sports reporter. He's flying over there next week to see this Zola Budd woman, the barefoot runner who wants to go to the Los Angeles Olympics and run for Britain.

"I'd already told him about you. I was hoping he'd drop in and see you. How far is Durban from Bloemfontein?"

They talked for a while, Dunnie rang off. Charlie was relieved to hear there was no subsequent click on the line. Mark Winter, the local rugby writer, came over. "Hi, Charlie Burton? I'm Mark…

how do you fancy coming with me to the rugby at King's Park on Saturday? I'll tell the Natal rugby guys the local soccer star wants to watch them play!"

Charlie grinned. "Love to," he said, "I'll meet you there."

The Mercury's coverage of Charlie and Solomon's story the next day was followed up by their rivals, the Daily News. Charlie was becoming something of a media star. He'd run home, without a tail, for another long chat with Piet and Sophie.

When he turned up on the Saturday with her, Mark looked a little taken aback. But after a brief hesitation, he walked them through the gates of the massive King's Park Stadium, where a large crowd had gathered to see the Sharks take on Eastern Province. A corner of the ground was filled with Indian and black fans. But the bulk of the supporters were white and well-heeled.

Mark led them up to a box high in the stands, where officials from one of the big sugar companies greeted them enthusiastically. They'd read all about the Englishman and his impact in KwaMashu. Celebrities were rare in Durban, and Charlie was worth knowing all of a sudden.

They greeted Sophie heartily too, perhaps imagining she was his lady in waiting thought Charlie, giggling to himself.

He and Sophie hadn't even kissed yet. But the chemistry was there. And they held hands loosely as two suited men guided them down the steps before the kick-off.

Charlie was shocked to find the pair of them led into the middle of the ground, with both sides lined up on either side of them. The public address system announced: "Ladies and Gentlemen, let's have a big Natal welcome for Charlie Burton, top scorer in the National Soccer League, and the hero of KwaMashu!"

The crowd rose to applaud Charlie, curious to see him holding

Sophie's hand, but happy to greet somebody prepared to risk the townships every weekend.

Back in the box, Charlie was subjected to all kinds of questions from the rich, influential businessmen who came to watch the rugby. The guy from South African Breweries wanted to know how they could get into the shebeens, if he thought it was worth sponsoring the big football clubs. The tobacco guys were eager to put their name to the main knock-out competition. The talk was of "the untapped market" and "a new middle class".

Charlie was full of ideas, very positive about the spending power of the average black man. But then he was a good waffler. The big wigs loved him. And Sophie began to talk to, recognizing opportunities. Realising, like Charlie, that big business might be a couple of lengths ahead of the rest of South Africa in accepting change had to come…and soon.

Natal were beaten, as was traditional at that time, and the crowd leaked away, quiet and acceptant, so unlike the township hordes. Charlie and Sophie kept talking, amazed they had enjoyed their day so much. Mark came up, his match report sent. "They loved you," he said, "Both of you. These guys aren't what you think they are. They want people to spend money. They don't care what bloody colour they are!"

Sophie and Charlie talked for hours about their day. About how capitalism might be a force for change rather than repression. Socialism sounded great, was easy to sell to the deprived… but the Communist system was creaking. Might have to shift to the right a bit! They couldn't wait for the argument with Vusi.

But then the chat turned to the resettlement camp. The haunting images. "Sophie, I've got to go back. Check on those twins. Will you come with me?"

"Of course Charlie," she said, gripping his hand, "But only if you score against Hellenic tomorrow."

They kissed then, long and deep, at Piet's place on the Berea. They looked into each other's eyes. And decided rampant sex could wait. For now.

They drove together to the game the next day, the small circle of friends. But the cops stopped them at the roadblock on the way into KwaMashu. And held them for 20 minutes before Inspektor bloody Moolman turned up. Charlie thought the end had come. He had a picture of the inside of a cell, electrodes, hose pipes, torture. "Englishman, you're surprisingly hard to find." He said. But he was smiling. "I was going to pick you up my boy. Scare the shit out of you. But I hear you made some interesting friends yesterday, you and your kaffir girl. They said she's bright. They liked you. You might be useful for my rich friends who look after our unofficial wages. Keep moving in those circles and we might just leave you alone. Any more clever business, any talk about the Trojan Horse and I'll pull you in, you can be sure of that. We're watching you Englishman."

He glared at Sophie and Piet and stomped off.

They drove on to the Princess Magogo. Huge crowd. White journalists in the press box for the first time. Television cameras broadcasting to both channels, SABC1 for whites and SABC2 for blacks.

A young white journalist came up to Charlie with a microphone and camera. "Can we have a word, Mr Burton?"

He pulled Sophie into the shot with him, clutching her hand. She flattened down his hair, pulled his collar up.

The cameraman laughed. "You're a brave one," he said in an Australian accent, "Don't they arrest you for that here?"

"It's okay," said Sophie, "His dad's from Upper Volta!"

Jabu was watching, carefully. Charlie gave a long, funny interview.

And stuck to football. He found the cameras no problem at all. He talked up South African football, said how much fun he was having, said the riot hadn't been that bad, he'd seen worse at Millwall. He joked about Natal's rugby-speaking predicament and suggested they should sign a couple of big Zulu props.

They lapped it up. The interview would appear on black and white channels. And his two goals against Hellenic, one a sensational first half lob from 40 yards, the second a typical power-header from a Prof corner, were written about in all the papers.

Piet hit a post from a Merv throw, Ace tucked in a rebound after a rasping shot from Charlie, Faya got a breakaway fourth in the last minute for a resounding win to open a gap at the top of the table. Jabu smiled. Mad-eyes glared. Sophie loved every moment. On the field, life couldn't have been better.

They left early the next morning. This time Charlie had his passport and they sailed through the border posts. The authorities hadn't tagged his identity yet.

They spoke long into the afternoon as they approached the area where Nkosana and Charlie had found the resettlement camp. But then they were stumped. The clinic had no name, the dirt roads all looked the same. Finally Charlie spotted some women walking with huge stacks of wood on their heads.

Sophie did the talking. They piled the women and their sticks into the hatchback of her Nissan. "These women have been to the clinic, they know Sister Michaela. They live nearby. They'll take us there."

The women loved being in a car. For the resettled, cars were an absent luxury. Nobody could afford a vehicle. It compounded the isolation of these lost people. In 20 minutes, they were driving up to the clinic, the lake looking even filthier than before, an awful smell drifting across a desolate scene. The women clambered out, took up their sticks and walked off. "They walk for days to find wood," Sophie explained. "We've saved them half a day at least. I don't know how they do it. Hardly any food and they carry a load of wood too heavy for me to handle."

They walked up to the clinic, through the listless, starving villagers, who looked at them with hollow eyes, empty stomachs, hands out in a begging reflex which had become part of their reaction to any stranger.

A new nun greeted them as they approached. "You must be the Englishman who came with Nkosana," she said, "I am sister Freda, from the Tyrol, welcome."

Charlie introduced Sophie, asked after the twins. "Ah, the twins," she smiled, "They are healthy and a handful! I don't think they know their mother is gone. The money you gave us and the help from the people in Port Elizabeth meant a lot to them, to all of us. Nkosana has been a great help. But we are worried the police got him last week. We haven't seen him for days. He is such a good man."

Charlie showed Sophie the five rooms of desperately sick refugees. It was shocking, horrific. Sister Michaela appeared. "Many have died in a week," she said, "We are getting desperate. Even with the money from you and Nkosana. We cannot carry on much longer."

Sophie pulled a wad of notes out of her purse. "This is from the Chaka Royals football club. We feel your pain. Please use it how you please. Your work is appreciated by all true South Africans."

"It's the AIDS," said sister Freda, carefully hiding the money in her bra, "The authorities say it is flu but we know it is worse than that. In Europe and America they say it is caused by injections and sex. Here they say it is God's way of wiping out the blacks."

Sophie grimaced. "We have seen this in KwaMashu too. People lose weight, they get sick easily, they cannot fight the infections.

Always it is the young, the women, the drug addicts. It is spreading fast. But nobody will act."

Then a horn. Charlie was amazed to see Solomon coming across the dry grass towards the clinic. With three white men following close behind.

"Solomon!" said Charlie, "How did you find us?"

"Jabu told me about the resettlement camp. We guessed you'd come here when Sophie said she was going away with you. These men have come to see you."

One of the suited, bespectacled guys stepped forward: "Neil Harris, Daily Mail," he said, "These are my colleagues. John Slade from the New York Post and Francois DuPois from l'Equipe in France. We want to know more about your time in South Africa, Charlie."

"Go inside the clinic, gentlemen. I think what you'll see in there will say more than any words."

They filed in. Solomon was hard at work with his camera. They spoke to the exhausted sisters… about death, about AIDS, about resettlement, about the authorities and their lack of help.

At last, thought Charlie, the truth will get out. The world will know what this government is doing to the lost people. He felt a hint of hope in his breast. Deeper, longer lasting than any goal he'd celebrated. As they walked, he told them about the Trojan Horse massacre, the scenes after the funeral.

Sophie gripped his hand hard. This place was killing her, breaking down the barriers within her. She was a proud Zulu, anxious for peaceful change. But this place, this stinking death-trap, cut through any arguments for gradual change, for patience. Something had to be done.

Then the twins burst upon them. Running through scenes of utter devastation, their little legs and bright eyes changed the nature of the scene. They were so alive while all around them death lurked.

Sophie and Charlie reacted spontaneously, picked up their prize pair of orphans, hugging them, spoiling them. Charlie pulled out the last of his hotel front-desk sweets, they were snatched with glee.

He could see Sophie was smitten too. While the journalists went about their mission, the four of them played happily outside, gamboling about, trying to communicate with broken half-words and gestures. Sister Freda admitted: "We can't give them the time we should. There are so many orphans, so few adults who can function properly here. It's hard to entertain kids when everyone is exhausted or starving… or sick."

While the journalists talked and Solomon ran through more rolls of film, Sophie coaxed the children into a few words. Xhosa was a click-filled language, but she knew some words… and the Nguni language she spoke wasn't that different. Like Spanish and Italian. They sat quietly while Charlie named the twins. "You," he said to the bouncing boy, "Are Jabu. Jabu Junior. And you, little Miss Cutie Pie, are a wonderful Lilly. Little Lilly. One day, I will come and take you away from all this. I will show you a land full of milk and honey. And football and dollies. Promise." Sophie translated, tears running down her beautiful cheeks. The twins laughed and leapt about a lot. The nuns stood off to one side and prayed that Charlie's words would come true.

A siren sounded in the distance, as it always did in South Africa when Charlie least expected it.

Their time was up. Sophie and Solomon urged the white folk back to the cars, there was a tearful, rushed farewell to the twins, more money pressed into the hands of the weary Sisters from Austria.

And they were away, with promises of a return "with plenty of stuff for the people… and the twins."

Solomon stopped, suddenly, in front of them. "There's cops up ahead, I can smell it. Here, take this."

He handed Charlie two rolls of film and the cards of the three journalists. "I've got some pictures too. We must separate, one of us may get away."

Charlie went to stop him. It felt safe enough, the sirens had gone quiet. And he could deal with any gnashing dogs. Then Sophie reversed, fast, slamming Charlie's door shut. A police car was coming over the rise ahead, all lights blazing, siren off.

Solomon roared forward and took a left, the coppers in hot pursuit. Sophie and Charlie went the other way, Sophie proving something of a Nigella Mansell, sliding around the gravel corners before eventually finding a way to the tar roads and some kind of normality. They didn't talk much. There wasn't much to be said. They both knew what had to be done. And it was life changing. Those two wonderful children couldn't be left there. No way. Not if it was the last thing they did. Together.

They drove through the night, arriving back in Durban on Tuesdsay morning, exhausted by their 24 hour crusade.

Piet met them at the door. "The cops have been round to the hospital. They're looking for me. I'm not going to work this week, told them I'm sick. But they'll find this address soon, and then we're in the shit. What have you done to wind them up?"

Charlie started to explain. Then remembered the rolls of film. "A chemist," he said, "We need to develop three or four copies of this film and send the pictures off to these newspapers. That's our priority. We'll talk on the way."

As they drove off, a large white car cruised slowly past the house. Sophie ducked below the dashboard. They weren't spotted.

"Naidoo," Charlie yelled, "He owns a chemist in town, he told me, we have to get there. They'll print these pix. They printed my t-shirt for Vusi's brother and I didn't even realise it was him. Naidoo's Pharmacy, it's in town."

As they drove, Charlie and Sophie explained to Piet what they'd seen, how the foreign journalists had witnessed the horrors of the re-settlement camp too. And Solomon had the pictures which would stop a weary world in its tracks.

They had to stop three times for directions to the Naidoo shop. They found it right at the top of the city, near the market. They were just opening… Ranjith was lifting the shutters, still favouring his ribs. Charlie explained quickly what they needed, what it was all about.

Naidoo grimaced. "You're getting in too deep Charlie. You don't understand what happens in this country. You saw what that mob nearly did to me in Soweto…"

A younger man stood at the counter. "What's up dad, what does this guy want… trouble?"

"Yup. This is Charlie, the English striker at the Royals. And this is Piet. They pulled me out of the mob in Orlando. Charlie's got pictures of a resettlement camp in the Eastern Cape. Blacks starving and dying. He only wants us to process them. And post them to the foreign papers!"

"You've got to help him dad," said the lad, taking control of the situation. "I'm Ashwin, I'm a bit more progressive than dad. I'll get the photographs developed. And I can do you one better than posting them here, where they might be checked on the way out of the country.

"My mate from university is getting out tonight. He'll post them from London when he gets there."

Ranjith frowned. "We shouldn't get involved, Ash."

"Dad, they've banned Hamed. He's got to leave all his family behind tonight. They've ruined his life just because he lectures sociology at Westville. They're after him for telling the truth. He'll do this with pleasure Charlie. Forgive my dad... he's old-fashioned. He thinks the Nationalists will look after us. He's wrong. They'll try repatriating us to Pakistan and Bangladesh, they'll take our land. That's what they'll do. I'm with you."

Charlie handed over the films and the journalists' cards, instantly impressed by Ranjith's articulate son. "Shit," said Ash, studying the cards, "You were with these guys? I just heard on the radio, they've got them under arrest with Solomon, one of the local journalists. These guys are in serious shit."

Piet, Charlie and Sophie were reeling. The police had got them. The four men were probably in a stinking cell in Port Elizabeth, being made to sweat, being made to talk.

Charlie felt responsible. "We split up, I thought they'd slip away. This is all my fault."

"No," said Ashwin, "It's the police's fault. The homelands policy. This stupid bloody idea they can hide all the blacks in the countryside and get away with it. These pictures could be the beginning of the end for all this. Once the world knows what the government are doing to these people, the United Nations have to get involved. It's wrong. Dad, you have to agree..."

"Okay, okay," said Ranjith, wincing from the pain in his ribs, "You do it. But Charlie you need to lie low. When pictures of resettlement camps and dying blacks hit the international press, BOSS will come after you. And you'll disappear quick."

"Here," said Ashwin, reaching into his pocket for some keys before scribbling down an address, "Go to this house. It's up in Overport. Safe house for people like us. Go there, I'll phone Dev and warn him you're coming. Nobody will rat on you to the security police there."

Satisfied the photographs would reach the right people, Piet, Sophie and Charlie drove back up through the city streets to Overport at the top of the Berea. Their new house was walking distance from the hospital, run by a lad called Devan, a huge bloke with the lump of a revolver inside his ever-present jacket.

He introduced the trio to their house mates, all scruffy looking, university lecturer types eager to keep out of the mainstream, away from prying eyes.

There were two spare bedrooms, both recently vacated when their eagerly-sought occupants fled to London to join the anti-apartheid activists who demonstrated daily outside the South African embassy, day and night, on Trafalgar Square.

This would be home from now on. Piet went back to retrieve their stuff and found his parents' holiday home ransacked. He'd taken all he could and run. Another door closed.

The chat in their new house moved things up a level for Charlie.

These were hard-eyed academic revolutionaries. Others came to visit. All were suspicious of Charlie and Piet... and awkward around Sophie. BOSS spent thousands every year funding students and lecturers to inform on their colleagues within the various left-wing organizations.

But somehow Charlie's football legitimised his presence in the group. He was the only person who actually spent time in the townships, dealing with the grass roots, everyday problems. Piet's hospital stories began to give him credence. And once they realised Sophie could talk the talk, they relaxed around her too. Thing is, how many whites, no matter how left-wing, really knew how to talk to blacks under Apartheid, thought Charlie in another eureka moment.

For once, this beautiful Zulu princess wasn't just a political gesture on Charlie's arm but a serious thinker in her own right...

with a far better grasp of what the future might hold for her people, for a country freed from Apartheid. The three of them became, in a few short nights, part of the surprisingly large left-wing community living on the edge of the two universities just outside Durban. People prepared to live different lives, think revolutionary thoughts. Charlie hadn't realised these people existed. He suspected BOSS weren't too happy about it.

Fox had moved the Royals training sessions to the nearby University athletics ground, under floodlights. There was too much going on in the township, too much going on around Charlie, to train at the Princess Magogo, to run the daily gauntlet of police road-blocks.

On Wednesday night, Charlie had a big decision to make. They were scheduled to play Durban City, a side which had dominated the old white NFL. They had twice won the multi-racial NPL but their crowds had dribbled away, commercial support for a "white" football club was feeble... and, like Hellenic, Pretoria's Arcadia and the other "white" sides, the end was nigh.

Problem was, with a full side out, they were still a threat. And they were run by an elderly businessman with rumoured links to the police force. If Charlie played and the imprisoned journalists had talked, he could be arrested at any point.

It was high risk, but Charlie knew he had to play. He turned up early at their ground, New Kingsmead, just over the car park from King's Park. Durban would make a great Olympic venue, he thought, taking in the two massive stadiums next to an athletics track, a 50m swimming pool and a cycling velodrome all within of a square mile, with the international cricket ground, Kingsmead, barely a mile away. Dlamini was already in the dressing-room. He showed Charlie a tiny pot filled with a vile-smelling purple goo. He sat Charlie down and, with a bit of help from Philemina, his not-unattractive daughter, he proceeded to massage the stuff into his head. "More muti, Dlamini?" groaned Charlie, "What have I done to deserve this? Is my hair bad magic now or have I got bloody lice?" Dlamini simply glared and carried on spreading the awful concoction all over his head, taking care to keep it out of his eyes.

"Now go shower, Charlie. Then look in the mirror."

He did as he was told. Towelled himself down. And leapt back from the mirror. His hair was beach-blonde, nearly bloody white. Philemina put the stuff on his eye-brows too. Carefully. Charlie was worried she was going to proceed on to the rest of his body hair... but she stopped at that.

"From now on, you are Bartholemew. That is a good name, no?"

Charlie laughed, realising what was going on. "Bart will do, Dlamini. They'll never catch me now!"

As they prepared for kick-off, the team all grinning at Charlie's bright new locks, there was a rap at the door. The Durban City chairman entered with a group of white men in suits and police uniforms.

"Ah Clive," he oozed, brandishing a photograph, "These gentleman have come up from Port Elizabeth, they're looking for this fellow. I told them I was sure you wouldn't be harbouring a criminal... but he does look a bit like that new English striker of yours."

Charlie took an instant dislike to the man. Clive had endured plenty at the hands of this bloke but it was Andy who spoke: "You bastard Ed. You don't bring the police into a football dressing room. You don't betray fellow footballers. What's this bloke supposed to have done? Let's see that picture."

The other guys sat quietly, heads down. Charlie was sweating. Andy looked at the picture. Then at the four high-ranking police officers from Port Elizabeth who had taken the call from Edward Griffiths and enjoyed their expenses-paid trip to Durban, complete with rooms at the Edward with a local woman thrown in.

One of the policemen spoke with a heavy accent: "We don't know this guy's name. The bloody kaffir Solomon took the picture but he wouldn't talk. He's paid for that. But the white journalists said they thought he was a footballer, an Englishman."

Andy looked around the dressing room. "Hmm. Looks familiar. This guy came to training a few times, but he never made it. Couldn't bloody head the ball." He said. "Looks like a coloured to me. Nobody like that here, pal."

The coppers, with Edward breathing over their shoulders, hoping to remove the Englishman from the ranks of the hated Royals, stared at their picture. They looked at the fifteen men sat around the dressing room. No dark, curly-haired blokes they could see.

"Ag Ed," said one of them, "You've wasted our time man. This isn't the guy those idiot journalists told us about. You've led us on a wild goose-chase, you doos!"

Griffiths reddened. Looked closely at Charlie. Jabu said quietly: "One more trick like this Ed and the wrath of my people will come down our your shoulders. These people don't belong in a football dressing room. Please take them up to your box, where they belong."

"You shut it kaffir," said one of the police. Vusi began to rise. Charlie held him back. "You? We know you Vusi Nkosi. And we know what happened to your Commie brother. You step out of line, you disappear. You hear me?"

With that the delegation departed. Dlamini did his damndest to lift the mood, his incantation reached fever-pitch. So did Clive's team-talk.

Jabu pulled Charlie aside: "Might be best if you don't score too many goals tonight. Edward will smell a rat. We're lucky those cops haven't talked to the local guys yet. But they'll put two-and-two together pretty soon. Be careful."

The team trotted out. City's side consisted of the best of the local amateurs and a couple of lads who, like Charlie, had come out for a winter of football from the lower echelons of British non-League football. If any of them had ever played against Charlie, they wouldn't recognise him now!

Having weighed up Jabu's advice carefully, Charlie came to a decision with his feet. Ten minutes in, Andy's long, hopeful free kick caught the Durban City defence square. He used his pace to accelerate away, took a touch and sent a rasping shot past their veteran goalkeeper, Alan Webb, who had kept a young Bruce Grobbelaar, soon to star with Liverpool in a European Cup Final, on the bench.

Webb got a miraculous hand to it and pushed the ball around the post. From the corner, Charlie found himself battered by about three defenders and the ball was safely cleared into the night sky.

That didn't help. Every touch they were getting stuck into him now. They realised this blond lad was the Englishman. Any confusion had quickly been cleared up on the pitch. Fortunately the gaggle of policemen hadn't stayed to watch the match. They'd buzzed off back to the Edward Hotel and another big night out on expenses.

While Edward Griffiths fumed in his box, alone with a couple of ancient hangers-on, Charlie became the focal point. Again and again he was brought down and George Thebe was in no mood for nonsense, booking a number of blue-and-white hooped defenders.

Charlie's time approached. Forty minutes on the clock. Teenage's flick on from Merv's throw found him on the bounce with two defenders pulling at Charlie's green shirt. He appeared to ignore the ball and turned his back but as he did, he flicked up a despairing heel, catching the ball as it fell behind him. It looped over his head, and dropped beyond the feuding trio. Webb saw the danger, advanced off his line… and Charlie, tripped from behind, stumbled and just got a foot under the ball as the goalkeeper fell on him at the edge of the box. The touch had been perfect. The ball lobbed over the goalkeeper, looped over the full-back behind him… and bounced on the line as the Royals fans, outnumbering the home support by 12,000 to 2,000, roared their approval. Once more, Charlie had struck before the break and the Royals were on their way.

City shocked the lot of them with a headed goal from a corner soon after the break but the Royals went back in front when Ace broke down the right and found Piet, on as a sub. Three City defenders had followed Charlie to the far post… leaving Teenage to nip in at the near post and toe Piet's inch-perfect pass beyond a bemused Webb.

Charlie made it 13 goals from six starts ten minutes from time to cap the night off nicely. Faya tore down the left, cut the ball back to Prof. He scuffed a first-time shot which was going wide until Charlie dived forward amid the flying boots to head the ball home. The Royals fans' celebrations could be heard well beyond the neighbouring rugby stadium and echoes of it would be felt in Soweto, where Kaizer Chiefs and Moroka Swallows were fighting out a 2-2 draw with serious crowd trouble and numerous injuries.

The Royals were now four points clear with two games to play in the League… and on Sunday came the JPS Cup semi-final at Kings Park, where a full-house 54,000 was expected for the arrival of Cape Town Spurs, a largely coloured side from the roughest parts of the fairest city in South Africa.

Jabu kept them calm. For all the shit going on in the background, the shootings, the riots, the police in the dressing room, this was a football team. And they were a game away from winning the league, three wins short of a sensational league and cup double, never achieved by a side from Natal since the inception of the NPL.

"Six games, six wins," said Jabu quietly in the dressing-room as the euphoria died down. "We've got the cops chasing Vusi and Charlie and we need to get through these last three or four games without any trouble.

"Keep your heads down. We won't meet until Sunday morning at King's Park. Be there at 10am. Our security men will be on the gates, the cops are refusing to police the semi-final. They want trouble. If we lose, there will be trouble. There won't be more than a couple of dozen fans from Cape Town, so we win and all will be fine.

"Then we take one more League game – but it's against Chiefs – and the final against them or Pirates. Time to concentrate boys. Stay out of trouble. Stay off the booze. Dlamini will know!"

At that moment, the door of the dressing room slammed open. The City guys stood there. Tension ran high. Then Rodney Charles, their huge coloured centre-half who had kicked Charlie all over the park, walked straight up to his English rival and held out a hand: "You were too much for me tonight, Burton. Fucking spot on China. Go on and win the double for Durban!"

The dressing room broke into a roar, dozens of fans waiting in the tunnel joined in the chant of "Usuthu" and Sophie broke through the throng to hug her man tight.

"Bloody hell, Dlamini, give me a break," said Charlie as the Sangoma rubbed his head from behind while he held Sophie close and chatted to the City players amid the hub-bub. "I don't need magic until Sunday."

Dlamini took his greasy hands out of Charlie's hair. There was a shout... and silence. Griffiths was shouting: "Arrest the blond. He's in there. He's taken foreign journalists to see a resettlement camp and he's talking shit about some shooting in the township. He's a bloody Commie, he's screwing a kaffir girl!"

Sophie slipped out of Charlie's grip, held her father's hand. Charlie stood there. The crowd all turned to look at him. Two coppers were with Griffiths, locals, sweating, nasty, guns drawn. Looking for the beach blond hair Griffiths had described to them.

They looked straight at Charlie, then past him. And leapt on Merv, the blondest man in the room. Dlamini pushed Charlie to one side, grabbed his arm and thrusting him out of the dressing room around the blind side of Griffiths and his policemen. "How…" He looked in the cracked mirror on the dressing room door, fleetingly as he scurried away down the tunnel and out into the night.

Dlamini hadn't just been rubbing his head to improve his muti. He'd been rubbing the red earth and urine from the dressing room floor into his hair, which was now a gingery-brown.

He could hear Merv shouting: "Get your fucking hands off me, I'm not a Commie!" as they leapt into Sophie's car and off to the safe house. Piet arrived an hour later. The cops had really laid into Merv, once one of Griffiths' favourites at City, but both sides had come to his aid. Reinforcements had come barging in… but found a wall of black and white footballers in blue and green to contend with.

Eventually BOSS had arrived, the Inspektor looked carefully at each player… and then ordered his men to leave. Surprisingly Merv hadn't said a word. Nobody had betrayed the Englishman. Griffiths, in his 70s, had no idea what had happened. He was raving about Englishmen and hair colour and Commies. The cops agreed the man was senile and drove off to find some blacks without stamped Pass Books to occupy the rest of their evening.

Jabu phoned the house. "Keep your head down Charlie. They're hot on your trail. I want you to go home but I know you won't. They'd probably catch you at the airport anyway. It might be time to take refuge in the Consulate."

"Last time they did that, the police raided the place," said Charlie, "Nowhere's safe. And if you think I'm not playing at King's Park, you can think again."

Jabu chortled, he loved the Englishman. He'd had all kinds of people on asking if he was for sale. Chiefs, Pirates, Swallows and Jomo again. And the Mercury had phoned. He'd given them some made-up quotes from Charlie and explained his new hair-style was modelled on the surfers along the beach front. "Charlie loves Durban so much, he wants to be a surf dude!" Charlie had told Fred. But the news on Solomon wasn't so good. The cops had been in asking about him at the Mercury and Ilanga, going through his files and trying to find evidence of an affiliation to the Communist Party or the African National Congress.

Jabu told Charlie about Solomon. His family were anxious. No news for nearly a week. Just a raid on the family home in Umlazi. Charlie was worried too... "There's nobody in the house tonight Jabu, normally there's five or six hippies smoking dope and talking politics. Tonight, nobody..."

Later, much later, Sophie slipped into Charlie's bed for warmth and comfort. They still hadn't consummated their relationship, though they felt all the right things. Later still, they heard the front door. Charlie got up. Dev was standing there, bleeding from the lip, his eye swollen, his shirt split from a full-blooded blow from a police sjambok.

"We were in one of the non-racial nightclubs down by the docks, one of the unofficial ones we all go to with the students. There were a group of cops from Port Elizabeth there looking for prostitutes to take home. We got into a fight, they called for reinforcements and they've arrested everyone. I got away. It was a hell of a scrap. I put down two of the cops, then I ran."

Charlie pointed out the link between his evening and Dev's. It was almost laughable to think of the four fat, sweaty cops from Port Elizabeth running into Dev and his mates. But it wasn't that funny. The long-haired lefties from the house wouldn't last five minutes in the cells at police headquarters on Old Fort Road.

Charlie went back to bed. He was elated about his goals, about the possibility of the double. About the chance of the resettlement pictures being published. And if they'd simply put the three white journalists on a plane home, they'd soon put words to the pix and the truth would be out. But that would bring more pressure here.

And then there was Solomon Phagate. Big, lovable Solomon. Just as he'd finally got his dream job as a football writer with Ilanga, the cops had got him. He was no Communist, no armed freedom-fighter. Just a journalist in the wrong place at the wrong time. And now he was probably lying on the floor in a stinking cell, hovering between life and death while the police interrogator bombarded him with questions... about Charlie...

CHAPTER 8: WINNING

"The lead cow, the one in front, gets whipped the most."
　　　　　Zulu proverb (South Africa, Swaziland)

Piet and Charlie turned up at King's Park alone. The cavernous rugby ground was deserted. Sophie was in KwaMashu, organizing the buses that would bring over 30,000 to the rugby ground close to the middle of the city. Umlazi would empty too for this one. The two Zulu townships would be united today as the Royals attempted to overturn the Spurs from Cape Town. In Soweto, Chiefs were preparing to play Pirates in front of 50,000 for the right to play the winners of this one in the final.

Spurs were hard guys, apparently. Many of them had been brought up in Mitchells Plain and the nearby coloured areas filled by the exodus from demolished District Six. Deprived of their traditional home near Cape Town, the move to drab townships with no facilities had encouraged crime and gang warfare.

South Africa's coloured population, caught like the Indians between black and white, suffered from chronic levels of alcoholism and, reputedly, the highest murder rate anywhere in the world... but the heady mix of races which ran through their veins produced sportsmen of great quality. From Basil D'Oliveira to Herschelle Gibbs, a kid who could run the 100m in under 11 seconds on grass, pop a drop-goal over rugby posts from the halfway line, but who would end up a Test cricketer. And that was after he had been ear-marked for a professional football career in England through an agent and former professional called Colin Gie along with lads like Quinton Fortune and Benni McCarthy, who would rise from the Cape badlands to star for Manchester United and Blackburn Rovers years later.

It was boys like these, tough, athletic, talented, black and brown, who turned up in the Cape Town Spurs bus, exhausted by a 20-hour road-trip along the tranquil but lengthy Garden Route and through the Transkei to the South Coast road Charlie had travelled a few times now.

The Royals had enjoyed a run-out on the pitch, which had hosted many memorable Springbok rugby internationals. It was a big thing offering the ground to the Royals for their semi-final. But Charlie had helped persuade the powers-that-be. They'd liked him. When Jabu had approached them, the Englishman was key to his negotiations.

Just that week, the Royals had crushed City at the football ground next door in front of nearly 20,000 and Charlie had been all over the local papers. Mark and Fred had enjoyed a feast of headlines as they put the paper together that week, "City gone for a Burton" probably the best of them.

The rumours of the police raid on the dressing room had swept the newspaper offices but nobody had written it. A mini-riot had broken out down near the docks later in the evening. In the end, the front page had been dominated by arrests and beatings. It was part of daily life around here. Cops were always after people, best not to ask too many questions or write too much about what they got up to.

Unknown to Charlie, Sophie had spent the morning getting the fans in early. And putting Vusi's men on the gates. They would recognise any policemen or their informers. The word would go out... and small mobs of supporters would conspire to keep them from the dressing room area where Vusi and Charlie were preparing with coach Clive's fiery pre-match talk and Dlamini's pre-match brew. "They've done the big coach journey," said Clive "They'll start slowly. We have to make sure we start strong, get on the board early."

The crowd was fantastic. Natal's rugby side, currently in a slump, rarely filled the place like they had in the old days. Today, with the boxes filled with white executives, the grand stadium was heaving with Zulus… and a surprising number of interested whites who had heard about their local side's sudden progression from possibles to probables.

The atmosphere was incredible. Capetonian fans were non-existent. Such was the luck of the draw. It would have been very different in the freezing rain and mud down there with 30,000 Capetonians to contend with.

Taking Clive's advice to heart, the Royals stormed forward from the off. Piet was making his first start. He put in a massive tackle in midfield and put Teenage through. The shot was weak, easily saved. The crowd were putting pressure on Piet. As a white face in the Royals, he had to produce immediately, Charlie knew that, recognised that this was Zulu territory. You had to earn the right to take a green shirt off one of the locals. Piet was up to it though. His parents had been calling, worried about the company he was keeping. His dad, a stockbroker in Johannesburg, had taken calls from the security police.

The hospital were worried about his timekeeping. The blacks loved him, they said, but there were problems…

Like Charlie, Piet used football… and cricket… as a panacea. Nothing could touch him when he had a ball to play with. Charlie went on a mazy run, pursued by Spurs defenders still stiff from their long journey. A two-hour flight had been replaced by a 20-hour drive because too many of them didn't have the papers for travelling by air. This would be their downfall.

Charlie played a one-two with Vusi, cut inside, beat a defender and the goal loomed large... but he looked up and glimpsed Piet making the run from deep. He dummied as if to shoot, the entire Spurs defence went right... and Charlie went left. His driven pass found Piet on the run and he produced a perfect side-foot finish from two yards. If the net hadn't been there to stop it, the ball would have gone over the stands.

If they hadn't been entirely sure of Piet before, the Royals fans were convinced now. Shouts of "Doctor" went up around the stadium. But Piet's goal served only to fire-up Spurs. Their lethargy was gone in an instant. They pushed forward in waves, hard to tackle, difficult to take the ball off. The Royals had possession for about 0.1secs before they'd lost it again, clearing their lines, struggling for air.

Charlie found himself dropping back as an emergency defender, sucked in by their constant pressure.

They hit the woodwork twice and Henry made one sensational save... but somehow the Royals got to half-time with their lead intact.

The huge crowd was quiet, worried. Their beloved side hadn't lost for six or seven games, but they'd never beaten Cape Town Spurs, who were probably the biggest threat to the Sowetan hegemony before the Royals' current surge to prominence.

Clive went bonkers in the plush, roomy rugby dressing-room. He tore into each player individually, accusing them of lacking backbone, letting the entire Zulu nation down and being single-handedly responsible for the evils of the modern industrial world.

Dlamini loved this sort of thing. Discipline was what these young warriors lacked. Clive hadn't given one of his coruscating, blood-on-the-wall team talks for ages. The Mad Eyes flashed, he threw a few feathers and a bone up in the air in a corner, then danced in the mud-and-urine sludge, fell flat on his face... and ruined the seriousness of the coach's Churchillian delivery.

Strangely though, it seemed to work. Still giggling over the sight of Dlamini's massive bulk falling headlong into the slurry, the nerves were dejangled pretty rapidly.

Right from the off, The Prof took the ball off their tiny midfielder, who looked like one of those desert-spanning bushmen who looked after the ball like it was an ostrich egg filled with precious water. The Prof's sizeable arise left him floored, he took the ball and kept it for the Royals, refusing to let the Spurs players rob him.

Then, when he had drawn three of the opposition into the challenge, he toed it to Vusi, who played it down the line first-time to Ace. The Wednesday-going-to-break legs blurred as he forged a path down the right wing. Then he appeared to stand on the ball and ran on into two defenders. Behind him, Piet took over, thumped the ball hard and low into the box. Charlie had over-run it. He turned and, body entirely off the ground, he produced a scissor-kick with his body levitating horizontally at about four feet. The connection was good, but the Spurs keeper somehow turned the ball onto a post. And there was Teenage to pop it in with a flick of the head. The entire mass of humanity exploded. A tsunami of noise could be heard as far as the coastal strip a mile away. Jabu put himself through one of those gut-wrenching 60-yard runs onto the pitch where he and Dlamini engulfed Teenage between a pair of ample bellies.

In the corner, the fans had leapt the fences, hardly touching the barbed-wire on the top, and thirty of forty of them were hugging Piet and Ace. And in the middle of it, with the stewards caught up in the moment, a small white guy in a bulky anorak ran up to Charlie and hit him in the face with a punch only a trained boxer could produce. He was pulling a glittering dagger of some kind out of his pocket when Dlamini saw the danger. He ran fully 20 yards at light-speed, smashed into Charlie's assailant. Others came running, the whole thing was chaos… Charlie slumped back on the floor, his jaw swollen and sore.

The referee's whistle eventually established some sort of order. Charlie got woozily to his feet. Nobody else had been visited by a would-be assassin on the middle of the pitch in front of 45,000 people. Just him. Of his would-be killer there was no sign. The ball was back in play. Charlie, rubbing his chin and offering a vote of thanks to Dlamini and his higher powers, pushed a simple one-two with Andy and got on with the semi-final.

The Spurs players refused to accept defeat. Ten minutes from time, the little bushman fellow, Daniel Ramakatse, dug a hole through the massed defence and finally found a route past the superb Henry in the Royals goal, toe-poking the ball home. Their celebration was an isolated glut of glee in the penalty area, but Spurs were still 2-1 down.

Charlie was urged back to win the headers by Clive. Andy McGeechan had gone off with a shoulder injury and Trigger Mulatsi, his big, earnest stand-in, couldn't win the aerial battles quite like the Scotsman, despite his 6ft 5in frame. Something to do with growing up using your feet, not rattling your brain, he always said.

Charlie did as he was asked, getting up to win two or three hopeful punts into Royals territory as time ran out. The big scoreboard showed 90 minutes, the Royals were creaking. Ace was on the floor, exhausted. Merv was bleeding from a cut above his eye. Charlie's mysterious assailant had left him with a grotesquely swollen face. His jaw felt out of place, dislocated. He could barely talk.

But the Royals stood firm. Until the 93rd and last minute of injury-time. A swift one-two between two Spurs players, a shot pushed out by Henry. Charlie went round behind the fallen goalkeeper as diddy Daniel hit a pile-driver over the prone custodian.

He was raising his hands to celebrate the equaliser, the crowd were already groaning... when Charlie threw himself headlong, unthinking, into the path of a leather missile flying at around 70mph. It hit him square on the jaw and, ever so slowly, looped up and over the bar. Game over.

Charlie was nearly unconscious as the fans negotiated the dangerous fencing again and lifted him to their shoulders.

He fingered his jaw gingerly. Bloody sore. But the ball had definitely put it back in position after the anonymous boxer's punch.

He kept a close eye on proceedings amid the hullabaloo, looking for the knife-carrying assassin. Then he saw a small group of white men, over by the side of the tunnel... heading for Sophie and the other wives and girlfriends. Charlie yelled from his vantage point atop the gaggle of fans. "Tokolosh!" he yelled, "Bad guys... there!"

The crowd transformed with worrying speed from celebrating football fans to a baying, monstrous mob. The knot of white men, clearly undercover police, ran for their lives, one of them pulling a revolver.

"Let them run," said Charlie, as they disappeared through a carefully crafted hole in the fence at the back of the car park behind the main stand, "Nobody can stop us winning the cup now!"

When the celebrations had eventually died down, Jabu, Dlamini, Sophie, Piet, The Prof and Vusi agreed it had been a genuine attempt on Charlie's life. "They would have achieved two things," said Jabu. "The man who has witnessed their Trojan Horse and their resettlement camp would have been gone. And King's Park would never have been used for football again, not after a player had been murdered by a fan in the middle of the pitch.

"It would have destroyed the whole image of South African football. Put us back years."

"Yeah, and Dlamini saved the day," said Charlie.

"No you did," said Sophie, "We're in the final, nobody can stop us now."

She went to kiss Charlie. He grimaced. "And hopefully you'll be able to use your jaw by then," laughed Piet, "I'll have a look at it later."

He turned to Jabu. "Listen, Jabu, I've enjoyed the last couple of weeks so much. Playing with your guys, talking to the fans. I want to set up a clinic in the township. A proper, free clinic. Would the Chaka Royals help fund the equipment? I'll cut the infant mortality rate in a month, sort out the stupid little disorders they won't treat in the big hospitals. Get some more doctors from Wits… maybe even get overseas funding and get to some of those resettlement camps…"

Charlie gripped Sophie's hand hard. In the morning, they were off again. The club had taken a call from a hysterical Sister Michaela. The police were taking the clinic apart. Then the line had gone dead. They had to go down and find out what had happened. But nobody could know. Jabu wouldn't let them travel, not after the attempted assassination, not with BOSS looking for him and Solomon still "disappeared".

The private party in the big bar next to the rugby stadium ended about 2am. Charlie wasn't drinking much these days. He stayed off it tonight, while the rest of the team – Merv and Andy included – sang and danced and joined the fans massed outside in their hundreds. How they would get home so late, with the railway station shut and the last of the supporters' buses long gone, who knew? But it wasn't a night to worry about details. The Royals were going all the way to Ellis Park, the home of South African rugby, where 100,000 would squeeze in to witness the final against the Kaizer Chiefs, the game of games, the end game.

Charlie knew it would be his last for the Royals. The net was closing. No amount of hair dye or safe houses were going to keep him out of the clutches of the cops.

He said a quick prayer. Just three more weeks and it would all be done. He would have paid Jabu back, fulfilled Dlamini's dreams... and he would take Sophie to England with him. Show her a country where the colour of your skin didn't matter... well not much. Surely the lads back home would welcome an exotic Zulu beauty. They wouldn't cause a problem would they? Something unsavoury stirred inside him. Was the average English male any better than the mustachioed Afrikaner when it came to race? Could he and Sophie settle safely there?

Not worth thinking about now. He hadn't really asked her properly. Or The Prof, her father, or Jabu, her uncle. The JPS Cup final and wrapping up the league were one thing. Avoiding BOSS was another. But persuading those two proud Zulus that Sophie should leave for England with him would be another task entirely. Mission Improbable.

Charlie was excused training until Wednesday with his jaw, which gave him and Sophie the chance to leave for the Ciskei the next morning, after they had read the papers.

Once more Charlie was the hero, though Piet got a few headlines. Teenage and Henry took up plenty of space at the back of the Ilanga, though their front page said something indecipherable about Solomon. Jemima, the lady who cleaned at the safe house, translated it roughly. Solomon's whereabouts remained a mystery. The three foreign journalists had been deported. Their embassies were complaining about their treatment at the hands of the security police.

Yet despite all that, they drove off down the South Coast road full of hope. Convinced they could find the orphan twins, save them from their fate. And give all the money they could lay their hands on to Sister Michaela and her brave fellow-nuns.

They stopped in Port Shepstone and Charlie hired a blue four-wheel drive Land Rover which might be mistaken for an official vehicle from a distance. He drove through the night, rubbing his jaw, feeling the nick in his ear, the wound in his buttock. He'd had more injuries in the last few weeks than he'd had in a lifetime. And most of them had come off the field. Sophie kept below the dashboard when they started to hit the dirt roads as the sun rose to herald a freezing dawn in the drab lands of the Eastern Cape.

Charlie eventually found some roads that looked familiar. And then he saw the lake... and the remains of the camp. And the burnt-out shell of the clinic. There was nothing left.

A few starving kids were wandering around, lost, hopeless. Two or three very sick women, probably pregnant, sat against the blackened wall of the clinic, hoping for a miraculous return of the all-healing nuns.

The little cemetery stood stark on the hillside. The huts were either wrecked or entirely removed. Probably to somewhere further off the beaten track.

Of the nuns and the twins... there was no sign. Charlie and Sophie were distraught. The few dozen villagers who had escaped the police-led clearance team obviously had no idea where everybody had gone.

They drove slowly around the area, in steadily wider circles. No idea how to track down the people they had travelled through the night to see.

They passed through a tiny dorp. A small knot of houses, a bar, two shops and three churches. He asked the white guy running the hardware store if he'd seen any nuns. Blank look. Sophie lingered in the background. She started a conversation with a handyman at the back of the shop. They talked, became animated.

Charlie waited outside, anxious, hopeful. "The nuns are in a safe place, Charlie. That guy says he's heard they're in a barn in a friendly farmer's place near Butterworth, a town an hour from here. Leave me. I'll find them. You must go home. You must go to training. Leave this to me. This is woman's work. A black woman. An Englishman with bright blond hair and a swollen jaw can't go to places like this. Too many eyes, too many suspicions, too much history."

Charlie was tempted to argue. To rage. He couldn't leave her in the middle of nowhere, like Andy and Merv had left him at the border post. But Sophie was having none of it. The handyman flagged down a mini-bus. Gestured for Sophie to come over. She looked beautiful. She walked like a sophisticated super model. But her eyes were sad. She had money, she was smart, she was sassy… but what would happen here, in the middle of nowhere, as she hunted down two orphan twins and three refugee nuns, probably wanted by the police for immediate disappearance before the story of their clinic hit the international papers… and journalists and television cameras swamped the area to find the starvation camps?

It didn't bear thinking about. Sophie clambered into the mini-bus. She waved as it roared away, driven by another of the great tribe of mad taxi drivers prevalent throughout the dark continent.

And Charlie wondered if he'd ever see her again. The drive back to Durban seemed endless. His jaw throbbed. His butt too. Fog descended on the coast road. Holiday resorts and beautiful beaches past by to his right, sugar cane and rolling hillsides to his left. This was God's own country, the south coast. And all Charlie could see was gloom as he nosed through the sea fret, wondering where Sophie was now, if she would survive this curious quest. Thoughts of this intelligent city girl among harsh, starving rural types scared the life out of him. She was beautiful, too beautiful to stay anonymous in tiny Butterworth. He pushed the thoughts out of his mind. Thought about the last two League games. And the Cup final. It worked. For about ten minutes he stopped panicking.

He swapped cars in Port Shepstone when the garage opened. He got back to the safe house around lunch-time. He slept, Piet turned up from his hospital shift and they went down to training at the University, where Jabu had a pack of spotters dotted around campus, checking for a police raid.

Away from his bigger concerns, the football provided welcome relief. Training was no longer spiky. It was intense, serious. Clive was on top of it all. Jabu's spies had compiled dossiers on the Chiefs team, their strengths, their weaknesses. By the end of the week, the Royals players felt like they knew each of the Amakhosi personally, every player, even the Chilean coach.

Charlie was supposed to be keeping his head down, but every day Jabu called with another request for an interview. Both he and Piet did pieces for the independent radio stations, 702 and Capital, and for the local papers.

Parnell Ndela, Solomon's mate, did a big piece on Piet Vermeulen for Ilanga, in Zulu. A lad called Grant Le Chat, a journalism graduate from the liberal Rhodes University in Grahamstown, interviewed The Prof for the Daily News. He produced a magnificent story headlined "From The Bottle To The Top" detailing Mlungisi Malekane's journey from alcoholism to professionalism. The first major feature on a black man the Daily News had ever published. And it dominated the back page, shoving rugby and cricket to the single columns inside. Charlie's life story, at least the footballing side of it, was all over the papers from Johannesburg to Cape Town.

He gave a good interview, revealing his thoughts on the surprising strength of South African football, the joy he got from the vast Zulu following, even a couple of quotes about "Mad-Eyes" and his role in the Chaka Royals' success. He even touched on his affection for a local lass in KwaMashu, gently pushing the barriers, and mentioned his concerns over what he had seen in the townships. No detail, not yet.

Clive Fox went public in the papers and on the television with his view that Charlie would be snapped up by a top English club on his return home. "There's no finer striker," he said, "Charlie is tough, good in the air. And he's got a nose for goal. I've never seen anybody strike the ball better. And the best thing? He's a super lad. The fans love him, black and white. I don't think he'll ever forget his winter in South Africa."

Too true. Charlie returned from training on Friday night to Dev, holding out the telephone. "Sophie!" he yelled. And she was fine. "Stop worrying Charlie," she laughed, hearing the anxiety in his voice, "I know how to walk like a common Xhosa countrywoman! I've found Sister Michaela and Sister Freda. But Mary, the third nun, had a heart-attack when they police started resettling the resettlement camp.

"All three of them took a beating when they tried to stop them burning down the clinic. Mary's in hospital in Port Elizabeth but she'll probably be okay. She's got to be nearly 60 but she's tough as an ox. When she's discharged, the police are going to put them all on a flight back to Austria. And there'll be nobody to look after the resettled people then. Nobody."

Charlie took it all in, sick inside. "What about Jabu and Lilly? Has anybody seen them?"

"We've got about a dozen orphans here in the barn, Charlie," Sophie explained, keeping him in suspense, "Jabu junior and little Lilly are fine. Too fine. They never stop playing and eating. They need a big strong man with stupid dyed hair to throw them around, to keep them busy. Can you think of anybody?"

Charlie's eyes welled up. He was about to launch into an over-the-top response, asking Sophie to leave this sick land with him in a fortnight... but the line had gone dead.

He hardly slept that night, planning for the next fortnight. Chiefs in the League at Kings Park on Sunday. Then up to Johannesburg for the final. Chiefs again, they'd beaten Pirates in extra-time.

Win both games, and the double would be done. The last League game became redundant. Charlie would be free to go home, though he would never really leave Africa behind him.

King's Park was full again on the Sunday. Sophie was still away. The hole in the fence had been fixed. Jabu's stewards had doubled in number. No more assassins. As Charlie roared through the gates of the ground in Sophie's Nissan, a white car flashed past. It had been following for a couple of miles, but Charlie hadn't noticed. Idiot. He had to develop eyes in the back of his head.

The crowd was even bigger than it had been for the semi-final. As always, the football fans managed to squeeze in an extra 10,000 on top of the rugby-watching capacity. The Zulus had no qualms about sitting in the stairways, squashing three into every two seats.

Charlie's arrival was greeted by huge cheers. He was a superstar now, pictured in every paper, featured even on the white news bulletins this week – and Shoot magazine in Britain had run him as a colour poster in his Chaka Royals gear, with a paragraph or two explaining how the lad from Fareham was taking South African football by storm.

Piet turned up. "The police stopped me outside the hospital," he said, "They wanted to know if I had seen you. They said they've been talking to my dad about the company I'm keeping. I said I only saw you at football, but I don't think they believed me for a second."

Charlie shrugged. They went out in the middle of the pitch. The roar from the fans was incredible. Chiefs fans had arrived by train early that morning and walked from the station, totally closing the dual-carriageway to the ground.

About 12,000 of them filled one end of King's Park, their repertoire of songs as loud and imaginative as anything you'd hear on the Kop at Anfield.

Their Sangoma came over to Charlie. "Good to meet you baas," he said, disarmingly.

"Ah, Caiaphas," said Charlie warmly, "I've heard all about you. Please don't call me baas, I'm just a footballer. You're the really powerful one around here!"

Caiaphas was shocked. The Englishman knew his name. He wasn't sure if that was a good thing in terms of muti, but he felt warm inside talking to this foreigner, which was rare.

He reached out as Charlie turned to speak to The Prof, attempting to snip a lock of hair for his cauldron. Charlie turned and caught him. With a smile, he took Caiaphas's scissors, chopped off a long length of dyed hair with black roots, and handed it to the Chiefs' Sangoma. "Caiaphas, you work for Kaizer Molefe, you can have all my hair if you want, and my toe nails. And this button off my coat. No charge!"

Caiaphas laughed, a high tinkling sound. He liked this Englishman. He would tell the Kaizer how clever he had been, getting so much good muti for the game from the much-feared Englishman. But did it count if he was so willing to offer bits of himself like this?

Charlie took off his Arsenal replica shirt. He'd had it for three years. Hadn't washed it for a week. He handed it to Caiaphas.

"Give this to your son," he said, "Tell him one day this team, Arsenal, will come here. They'll shake hands with Nelson Mandela and play against the Chiefs. I can predict these things!"

Dlamini had watched every moment of their bizarre exchange. He glowed. The Englishman had learned so much about Africa and the ways of the folk, most of it from him, Dlamini, the man who knew everything.

He put a protective arm around the muscular striker as they headed back to the dressing-room.

The Kaizer intercepted them. Tall, elegant, well-dressed. He had spent years in the States, playing with Pele, Beckenbauer and Marsh, all the greats. He'd named his side after the Kansas City Chiefs. And he needed a good old-fashioned English centre-forward.

Charlie knew what he was going to say: "I've turned down Mr Nkomo and I'll have to say no to you, Mr Molefe. But the Chiefs will do well without me. You have a great side here. Just wish you could play in the African Cup of Champions."

"I know," said Kaizer, "It hurts when you see the rest of the continent playing football and we can't join in because of our government. One day..."

"You should send your son to school in London," said Charlie, "I'll keep an eye on him. They have some great schools..."

Kaizer looked back. "And what, bring up an English son who has to live in Africa?"

"It could be worse. He'll have self-respect, the kind of dignity Apartheid takes away from your youngsters. If I was an African kid, I'd be out throwing stones every day. Get him away from all this. He'll come back strong, with knowledge of the real world."

Charlie's conversations with the Chiefs owner and their Sangoma somehow took the wind out of the sails of their pre-match rituals.

While Jabu, Clive and Mad-Eyes held the Royals in their grip with a series of Gettysburg-strength addresses, the Chiefs were somehow lost. They were expected to win. They had money, a huge fan base, average crowds of 40,000 wherever they played. These Royals should be flushed.

But right from the whistle, the Zulu side looked the more confident of the two. The Prof was imperious, but they'd expected that. One of their two teak-tough Argentinians was quickly dispatched to deal with him. Piet intervened, accidentally crashing into the huge Latin American, who had thighs like a buffalo.

Pedro Goncalves spat in Piet's face, but the South African simply looked right through him. "Touch my friend Prof and I'll rip you apart," said Piet, who had arrived at the ground in his national service uniform, "I run the army in South Africa."

Goncalves reigned in his competitive instincts instantly.

All this gave Charlie room to manoeuvre.

The Chiefs were no mugs, but Charlie had a lot to get out of his head. He wanted the ball so he could forget about Sophie, Jabu Junior and little Lilly. Forget about BOSS and guns and death and funerals.

He demanded it, craved possession. And he got it. Rather than playing as a conventional centre-forward, Charlie found himself filling the hole just behind Teenage, making the play, prompting his side forward, spreading the ball.

It threw the Chiefs centre-backs completely. They'd expected a free-running striker, eager to turn them, catch them square.

Instead, they found themselves uncertain, having to leave their comfort zone and try to get to Charlie before he popped perfect first-time balls to all corners.

Their coach, Mario Tuani, was a legend in South Africa. A Chilean dictator who had turned to football. One of the few foreigners who thrived on the politics of it, the endless shenanigans.

He told his centre-backs to sit back, soak it up. Stop trying to move up to Charlie, who was lying deep and spreading the play. So they did. Charlie got the ball and ran at them. They backed off... and backed off. Charlie unleashed a shot from just outside the box and the Chiefs goalkeeper, reputedly the best in South Africa, just stood and watched as it flew past him, inches wide of the goal.

The Royals had several more chances, but for once there was no goal just before the break. As they trooped off at half-time, amid a wave of cacophonic noise, Charlie put an arm around the great Chilean godfather and said: "Just let them play, Mr Tuani, let them loose, these are African footballers with great skills. You're stifling their natural talent."

He walked off before Tuani could reply. His team talk was confused, diffident. Clive Fox's wasn't. It was a torrent of positivism: "We've got them on the rack," he smiled, "I've never beaten the Chiefs before. Now is the time. Seize the day boys…!"

What the lads made of that one, Charlie wasn't sure. But Dlamini whispered in Charlie's ear: "Carpe diem, my boy, carpe diem."

They did. The Prof got the first, a rifling free-kick after Charlie had been pulled down outside the box. Charlie ended his mini-drought with a header from an Ace cross and Vusi finished it off with a 50-yard run and exquisite finish. Too many confused Chiefs, not enough Indians, it appeared. A thumping 3-0 triumph.

The League championship trophy appeared by helicopter after the final whistle. Officials from Johannesburg in their suits and ties emerged and added green ribbons. The Prof and Andy lifted the trophy together. The roar swept reality into the Indian Ocean.

The celebrations went on long into the night. Charlie was interviewed again and again. "Fourteen goals in eight games, how do you feel?" was the eternal question. He told them. "Bloody brilliant! But this is about playing for the best team in Africa, it's not about the boy from Fareham. These lads are the best, every single one of them."

"And the double?" Charlie chewed his lip, massaged his still-painful jaw. "The Chiefs won't be this easy at Ellis Park," he conceded, "But we've got the team to do it. To break the Soweto monopoly once and for all."

Jabu was a media star too. The persistent woman from US television interviewed him, the BBC world service got a microphone under his chin. Jabu talked and talked. About Charlie, about Piet… about his local lads. And Merv and Andy, his "great white hopes".

"I had a dream," he told them, sounding for all the world like African football's Martin Luther King, "Of a team of all colours, all talents. And that dream is coming true."

Charlie was taken home in a madly-driven taxi. He hunkered down in the back, in case the police were watching. Tuesday they'd leave for Johannesburg with the League trophy. He had to stay free until then. Two more days.

In the safe house the next day, Charlie took a call from Sophie. The line crackled. "We've moved," she said, not as cheerful as before, "The police have sent Sister Michaela and Sister Helga home. Sister Mary died in hospital. The doctors wanted to say the police killed her, but they were persuaded not to. I've got Jabu and Lilly. Your friend Nkosana Poti is sheltering us in New Brighton. I'm alone now Charlie, and I'm scared."

Charlie tried to remain calm. "You've got to get to Johannesburg, Sophie. It's our only chance. I'll try to book flights to London for the four of us… but without passports…"

Sophie was crying. "Nkosana says three international newspapers published pictures of the resettlement camp and the clinic yesterday morning. They said an English footballer had stumbled across the place. Nkosana says BOSS won't let you get away with this. They will hunt you down. But he says you did well… the world will take notice now."

Charlie sighed. Wondered if anyone would really care. Would

Margaret Thatcher and Ronald Reagan stop their quiet trading with the Apartheid nation now they had proof of the devastation, the sickness going on? Would they announce real sanctions against a country rich in gold, platinum and packed with nearly a million whites with the right to British passports? Of course not. There would be an outcry and everything would go back to normal. Public disapproval, background co-operation. Same old, same old.

And what would this mean to him and Sophie? The word was out. Even the local papers, the Natal Mercury, Ilanga and the Daily News had picked up the resettlement camp story by the next day. The SABC news was claiming the international press had, as normal, distorted the facts. A Government minister came on and talked about "Communist conspiracies" and claimed the clinic was simply "over-run" during a flu epidemic. And that the government had since cleaned the place up, sorted things out. The Ciskei, said the minister, provided unemployed Xhosa people with their own nation, a rural community in line with their history, where they could live with dignity.

Charlie felt like throwing up. Overseas, he knew the three journalists, shaken by their experience at the hands of the local authorities in the Eastern Cape, would dig away at the situation. Would probably find the nuns in Austria when they got back. But would it really change a thing?

Now Charlie had to leave this divided land… but first, Ellis Park, the Cup final. No matter what.

CHAPTER 9: FLIGHT

"If you provoke a rattlesnake, you must be prepared to be bitten by it." Gikuyu proverb (Kenya)

The trip to Johannesburg was uncomfortable for Charlie. Jabu had one of his madly-driven taxis take him to the station. He travelled by train, a sleeper, click-clacking through the tiny stations which dotted the rail network on the way to Egoli, the city of gold, Johannesburg.

It was a strange journey. Beggars lining the route through the forested hills outside Pietermaritzburg. Snow in the Drakensburg mountains. The urban bustle of Johannesburg's main station. With his football boots clutched in his hands and his small bag of possessions slung over his shoulder, he found The Prof in the ticket hall.

They drove through the busy streets, the endless traffic lights, to Wits University and their little stadium nestled under the main motorway.

Charlie relaxed the moment he saw the rest of the lads out on the field, training with Fox. A surprising number of fans and journalists surrounded their session. Applause broke out when Charlie trotted up, changed and ready to prepare for the biggest game of his life so far. The jaw was nearly back to normal, the hair still had a long, long way to go.

Afterwards, some of the journalists approached him and asked straightforward football questions. Two or three hung back, nervous, casting glances over their shoulders.

When he had finished talking about the game, his hopes, his double dream, how much he owed Jabu and Clive, the non-sports journalists sidled over.

An American from UPI went straight to the point: "Are you the British soccer player who found this resettlement camp in the Ciskei? What was it like? How many bodies did you see? Have you ever seen anything worse than that in your life?"

Charlie sighed. "Guys, I had the misfortune to stumble across a piece of hell on earth. If I talk about it in detail, you know what will happen to me. Give me a break. Come see me after the Cup Final on Saturday. Until then, I can't say much. Just look at the pictures, read what the journalists said. Not everything in this country is bright and sunny. There is a darkness at the heart of this nation and I've seen it, several times. If you want some reference points look at Chile under their military junta. Censorship, imprisonment without trial, no juries, police immunity, a government running wild. Only here, you can't hide. If you're the wrong colour, you're guilty."

He'd gone too far. Those words were winging around the world by dinner time. Hungrily devoured by editors in offices from New York to London, Paris to Addis Ababa.

Still, getting it off his chest a bit had helped. Charlie ate his meal at the Milpark Holiday Inn next to the Wits ground with gusto. Bollocks to them. He had to survive a couple of days. Jabu had heard Sophie was safely on her way from Port Elizabeth. He had booked flights, they'd have to try to sneak the twins through on one of their passports. Sophie and Charlie were booked on British Airways to fly separately on the same flight with one child each. If he could just get into the air, his problems would soon be over. He'd be in a country where he didn't have to look over his shoulder all the time. God, he missed Sophie. She'd make it all better.

The cops turned up for training the next day. Jabu and the Kaizer himself had put people around the ground but the police, some in uniform, the more threatening-looking ones in safari suits, pushed their way in, shouting and swearing.

They stopped training. "Where is the man in these photos?" demanded the biggest of them. "We have been told by our bureau in Durban he plays football for this team."

Once more, they scanned the team... and saw no Englishman with dark, curly hair. Only 12 black men and three white guys, none like the swarthy Commie in the picture. Merv came under scrutiny again. He surprised them all: "Look officer, that guy was training with us, but he was just one of those Commie trouble-makers. He's back in London now. He's probably demonstrating in Trafalgar Square today with the ANC. I fought guys like that on the border, I still do my camps with the army reserve. I wouldn't have him here. He's run away, like all the other Commie bastards."

"You sure? You want me to take you in for questioning?" said the BOSS man. "We can make things very uncomfortable for you."

"Listen," said Merv, "My dad is Stan van Tonder. He's the brigadier for the force in Heidelburg. Broederbond all his life. I know what I'm talking about. If I see another trouble-maker like that, I'll call you. Moenie worry. I might play football with these people, but I don't want them running the country. No way."

The cops seemed satisfied, assuming yesterday's quotes from somebody here had been manufactured by desperate foreign journalists. Liars all of them.

Relief all round as the knot of officials drove off with a squeal of tyres. Back to training, chatting, focusing on the task ahead. Charlie felt like two people. One caught up in the awful politics of this nation, the other a footballer with only one goal. And he'd forgotten what he looked like with his natural hair colour.

And so Saturday dawned. Charlie sat with Merv and Vusi in the back of the coach. Their pre-match discussion had ranged from police brutality to marking in the box. The pair were nearly capable of holding a proper conversation. Everybody had been impressed by the Merv's conviction under interrogation at training. Nobody else in the squad could have convinced the police quite as easily. Merv shrugged: "I want the win bonus! Don't think I suddenly like all you grubby lefties, Charlie. You think you know best, but this country can't go one-man, one-vote. It will be a blood-bath..."

Fortunately, as Vusi cleared his throat for a robust response, they pulled in behind the dressing-rooms at Ellis Park, the biggest stadium in South Africa.

Charlie was ushered first into the dressing room by a smiling Jabu. He stopped the others and closed the door. As he walked in, through the now-traditional mud-and-urine sludge, he was hit painfully in the groin by two missiles. One was called Jabu, the other Lilly. Charlie fell to his knees, scooped the orphans up, one in each arm, and went head to head with the love of his life, glowing in the middle of the dressing room.

"You are my queen," he said to Sophie, who beamed back: "Then this is your prince... and your princess. I'm amazed they recognise you with your hair like that. It's awful!"

The rest of the team gave them ten minutes to catch up. Sophie had been with well-connected people in Alexandria overnight. The police had manned the airport and checked the Royals flights. They put road-blocks all over the place on the Durban road. But they hadn't checked the trains. Blond Englishmen never caught trains in this country, unless it was the luxurious Blue Train to Cape Town. And the journalists hadn't actually named Charlie in their resettlement tales, which had reignited the whole Apartheid debate.

Somehow, they were still free. Sophie took the twins up into the Royals box. Clive and the squad entered the dressing room.

Excited but quiet. Word was the Chiefs had signed an English goalkeeper, who would play under an assumed name. He was from one of England's big first division clubs and nothing would be said. Chiefs had that sort of influence at the top of the game in South Africa.

Clive took them through their responsibilities. Dlamini hummed in the background, gently tweaking their luck, encouraging deities to look kindly on the great Zulu crusade which would end here, in front of nearly 100,000.

They went out and had a look at the ground. The surface was as good as any Charlie had played on. The ref, George Thebe, smiled as Charlie approached: "Englishman, I hear you are in demand, our government's police force have asked to see the team-sheet. They're looking for a swarthy man with black, curly hair. I said they have millions to choose from!"

Charlie laughed, shook Thebe's hand. "George, just give me a fair crack of the whip today, it's my last game. Then I go back to London and tell everyone what's really going on here."

George had never really got on with the foreign footballers before. They tended to sneer at him, lack respect. Charlie's eyes betrayed no such slurs. Here was a man with a good heart and strong legs, thought George, a man I can respect.

Charlie watched while fans from both sides ploughed their crazy path through the opposition ranks, emerging bloodied over the perimeter fence to take the applause before being hauled away by the stewards.

Years later, 34 people would die in a crush at this stadium, overloaded for a game between Chiefs and Pirates. But Ellis Park would rise again, returning to host World Cup games while Soccer City would bloom near Soweto, a stadium extended to host a World Cup final and 94,000 fans in proper seats.

But for now, Ellis Park, the home of Transvaal's rugby lions, would do. And 100,000 would pack into a stadium with a capacity of 75,000 to see if the upstart Zulus could indeed batter the Amakhosi, the Chiefs, as they had a week ago, when they clinched the league title with a 3-0 win.

The Royals filed in to get changed. The Chiefs, in expensive tracksuits, were heading out to look at the pitch. One of them swore at George, Charlie stepped in: "You watch your mouth mate, treat the referee like your father. With respect."

George glowed, the Chiefs glowered, furious at the Englishman's cheek. In their midst stood a tall white man, gloves in hand, talking to no-one. Charlie fixed him with his best Friday-night-in-Fareham-and-you-don't-scare-me glare.

The goalkeeper looked at the floor. "Mercenary," muttered Charlie, so he could hear.

Dlamini tied the ribbons carefully around each player. The twins popped in and were given tiny muti-soaked mementos of their own, as was Sophie. Any extra ounce of luck from the calabash could be vital.

It was The Prof who spoke last, before they filed down the tunnel for the national anthem and the kick-off.

He said: "In all my years boys, I have never played for a side like this. It's magic. Shit, I'm even starting to like Merv! Let's get out there and do this thing. For Jabu, for Clive, for fucking Mad-Eyes… and for the Zulu nation. Usuthu!"

No more motivation was needed. The Prof led them out, Andy behind him. The crowd bellowed, surged, sang.

The national anthem began once the two sides were lined up opposite one another. Nobody sang. This was the language of the oppressor. A song for the dominant population group, about their struggle for power with the English.

As it ended, Charlie pulled the team into a huddle. He only knew the first few words of the real anthem. But he bellowed it amid the hub-bub: "Nkosi Sikelele Africa..."

Soon the team had taken up the soulful tune. And then the Chiefs players, stunned, joined in. And finally it swept around the crowd... loud, proud. A song banned by the authorities, sung here, in one of the temples of Afrikaner rugbydom.

Jabu was shaking his head up in the box. "That boy Charlie, he's trouble!" he smiled, and looked at Sophie. "You're going with him aren't you Sophie? You will be lost to us."

"Never, uncle Jabu. Charlie has Africa inside him now. The twins will always be African, I will always be African. We will visit when we can. And one day, when the revolution comes, we will be back. You know that."

"The revolution?" Jabu laughed. "They've hushed up the deaths and the disappearances for years. The world doesn't even act when it sees those pictures of our people dying in the Ciskei, like some concentration camp. It's a holocaust and they're ignoring it. Trying to explain it away. There will never be a revolution. Just more shootings, like KwaMashu last month. And nobody cares."

"Charlie cares," said Sophie quietly. "He'll prove it to you on the pitch today, and then he'll prove it when we get to London. You mark my words. One day we will be back and you will live in a big house in the city and we'll remember these times like an old nightmare. A ghost of the past."

Out in the middle, surrounded by a wall of noise, Charlie kicked off, giving a short ball to Teenage, now nicknamed "The Head" for his recent flurry of vital, headed goals.

The Chiefs, in bright gold, were a lot happier up at altitude. Johannesburg is about 5,000 feet above sea-level, making breathing difficult for those accustomed to coastal living. Charlie hadn't really noticed it before. Perhaps his focus had been on the twins and Sophie rather than the climax of the football season.

He struggled to get into the game. So did most of them. And when Charlie finally had a chance on the half-hour, his powerful header from Merv's throw was saved comfortably by the mercenary goalkeeper, so sure of himself, so arrogant.

The Chiefs worked hard to break down the Royals defence but Vusi – who had been called in for questioning and roundly beaten by the police four times in the last fortnight – stood firm next to McGeechan and Van Tonder and Mulatsi. Even when they found a chink of light, there was Henry – who would one-day become a film-star, playing Chaka himself – to deny the Amakhosi.

But under such pressure, something had to give. Caught by the length of the goalkeeper's industrial-strength boot, Merv and Andy were left flat-footed by the pace of the Chiefs centre-forward, a lightning quick sprinter called Peter "Terror" Mathebule, plucked from a team of miners two years before. He'd run the 100m in 10secs flat on grass and barefeet at Durban Deep mine's sports day, so how were two big centre-backs supposed to stop him? Henry was comprehensively beaten, the ball passing between his legs… and the Royals went in 1-0 down to a wall of noise from the Soweto fans, blowing horns and bellowing.

At half-time their manager, the godfather Tuani, shrugged as Charlie passed: "I thought you were a player, I was wrong…"

Jabu came straight over to Charlie in the dressing room, before Clive could get stuck in: "I know there's a lot going on in your life Charlie, but this is it. This could be your last game. Please man, pull yourself together. The twins are up there and Sophie wants to show them what you can do. You're letting us all down."

Clive said much the same. He went from player to player, berating each individual. When he got to goalkeeper Henry, the poor man tried to pre-empt the attack. "I know boss, I should have kept my legs shut."

"No," said Fox, furious, "Your mother should have kept her legs shut."

The old joke didn't even raise a titter. Dlamini grumbled and grimaced in the corner. Charlie snuck out before the rest of the team. Took a few balls and ran on, alone. He rolled the first ball out in front of him, cracked it sixty yards into the net. He pushed the second ball forward. Repeated the trick. And the third. The Royals fans screamed and yelled, the Chiefs fans cried foul. This was bad muti, strictly not permitted according to the laws of African football. Caiaphas emerged. The Chiefs' Sangoma acted just as the crowd were getting out of hand, rattling the fences. He put an arm around Charlie, hugged him. The atmosphere eased instantly. The rest of the players were coming out. Round two. Bring it on, thought Charlie, waving up at the executive boxes, hoping Sophie and the twins were somewhere in that direction. He spotted Dlamini, who mysteriously held up three fingers at his Englishman. Charlie wondered if it was some sort of rude African gesture he hadn't yet come to grips with.

Tuani was astonished as Charlie dominated the early stages of the second half. Once more he had dropped back in the hole, demanding the ball, dictating the play.

The Chiefs were run ragged, trying to pick up the new white guy, Piet, who had come on at half-time, trying to restrain The Prof, Ace, Teenage. And for once the ref wasn't letting the Amakhosi get away with anything. Every foul was pulled up, every handball spotted by a diligent Thebe. This game would be won fair and square.

And from one of those honest free-kicks, The Prof sent a long, looping ball into the box. Charlie rose highest, half an eye on the emerging English goalkeeper. Instead of powering the ball towards him, he pulled it back, across the goal. And there was Teenage to head it goalwards. Somehow the keeper scrambled back to produce a stupendous diving save to his left, the ball looped up in the air and Charlie got on the end of it, ramming an unstoppable equaliser over the mercenary's prostrate body.

Ten minutes later, Charlie found space outside the box, Vusi cut in from the right and pushed the ball along the immaculate turf. Thirty yards out, Charlie absolutely thwacked it, the perfect drive. This time the keeper could get nowhere near the sizzling sphere... and the Royals were ahead for the first time.

His third was inevitable. A mazy run from The Prof, who looked up amid the flying boots, flipped the ball over and Charlie caught it gently in his instep. He deftly lifted the ball up and onto the back of his neck, then let it drop behind him. The two defenders had no idea what to do. Mesmerised, they watched as he heeled the ball back over his head, beyond them. Then Charlie ran on to the bouncing ball and crashed home the hat-trick.

It was all over. The Kaizer sat with his head in his hands. Beaten. Comprehensively.

The final whistle blew, the stadium erupted. The Chiefs, as one, came to shake Charlie's hand. The aggression, the pride, had drained away. It had been replaced by a grudging respect. Kaizer strode up, head high: "I paid that bloody goalkeeper millions to keep you out. You were too good. Next season, you're here. I'll give you money, sports cars, women..."

"You know my answer, Kaizer," grinned Charlie, "No deal! And I've got the woman of my dreams already!"

Then Molefe hugged him. And whispered in his ear: "Don't go in the dressing room. The cops are there. They've rumbled you. My people will keep them there... you need to get away."

That was easier said than done. Microphones were being pushed into his face, journalists crowded around him in the tunnel. It was time. The hat-trick had served its purpose. He had centre-stage.

"How did that feel, Charlie?" asked the man from the BBC World Service, "The Pompey reject from Fareham scores a hat-trick to win the cup in front of 100,000 Africans. What now?"

Charlie cleared his throat. "Listen up, I can say this only once. The police are waiting to arrest me. All of you. Hush." A silence fell. "I can only tell you what I have seen in two months in South Africa.

"This is a wonderful country. Great people. They have welcomed me with open arms, warm hearts, friendly shebeens. But there is a sickness, a serious sickness in this nation. And I think you all know what I'm talking about. Apartheid. Yes, apart hate.

"I came here to play football, I didn't come to South Africa to witness the atrocities I have seen here. To live normally in this country, you have to have both eyes shut.

"I have seen my friend arrested and beaten for playing football on the beach in Durban. His crime? He was black. I have seen people whipped for sitting on a bench. The problem? It was a white bench. But it gets worse. That's just petty-Apartheid.

"A week after I landed, I was in KwaMashu and I witnessed the police shooting women and children with automatic weapons. For throwing stones. The cops called it a Trojan Horse operation. They hid behind boxes on a truck, then opened fire on everyone. They killed dozens, but not a word appeared in the papers. The security police hushed it all up, they arrested people in their hospital beds. Then they tear-gassed the funerals and beat the hell out of the mourners.

"There's more. A few weeks ago, as some of you may have read, I stumbled across a resettlement camp in the Ciskei. The scenes I saw there will stay with me forever. People picked up and dumped in the middle of nowhere, left to die, looked after by a couple of nuns, they are dying, even now, in their dozens.

"And again, they tried to keep it quiet. Tried to stop the truth getting out. One of the nuns died after a beating. The other two have been deported. Now there is nobody to care for the lost people of that nameless place. There is a dreadful story to be told about the real South Africa. Margaret Thatcher might ignore it, but the British people need to know… this country is another Nazi Germany. Ordinary people are made to feel like aliens in their own land, they must struggle against poverty and discrimination… they have no choice, they cannot change the colour of their skin.

"Nelson Mandela is the only man who can rescue this great nation from the horrors of Apartheid, I implore you, act now, free Mandela, put pressure on this government, make them aware of…"

At that point, policemen started to emerge down the tunnel, grabbing journalists, pushing cameramen to the ground. Their long, leather sjambok whips were whistling as they came.

Charlie turned and strode back out onto the pitch, where the players were gathered for the trophy ceremony. The head of South African football was giving a short speech.

As Charlie approached, he turned to the blond Englishman and said: "And the JPS Man of the Match… Charles Burton!"

Charlie took his trophy and an envelope. Then they turned to Mlungisi Malekane, The Prof. "And the JPS trophy leaves Johannesburg for the first time… the winners… Chaka Royals!"

The Prof lifted the cup. The still-packed stadium rose as one. They played Stevie Wonder on the sound system but it was soon drowned out as the real anthem echoed around the stands. Jabu was in tears, Vusi ran over to hug Charlie. Sophie struggled over with a twin in each arm. Magic.

In the background, the police were struggling to get past the stewards, who were telling them: "We have to keep the crowds back, you cannot go on the field of play, baas!" They couldn't risk drawing their firearms with television cameras everywhere.

The players lined up and took their medals, one by one. Charlie handed his to Dlamini, who was moist-eyed, alone and nearly overcome by emotion. He gave him the Man of the Match envelope, with a cheque for a substantial sum.

As Charlie hung his medal around the Sangoma's neck, Mad-Eyes turned and gestured to a small gate on the other side of the ground. Then he whispered: "You must go now Englishman, there is a man who will drive you to the coast. You must take the woman and the orphans. But we shall meet again."

Sophie had appeared out of nowhere. Charlie, still in his sweaty Royals strip, grabbed the twins. He carried Jabu and Lilly across the pitch and the crowd went mad, thinking this was some kind of celebration lap. Charlie waved as best he could. Lilly and Jabu waved too, Sophie raised both hands. The photographers thought it was all for their benefit, snapping away.

Then they passed through the far gate and into the bowels of the stadium. Two or three men with bandannas over their faces pointed the way. The four fugitives were hustled into a mini-bus. The customary mad-man sat at the wheel. In a squeal of tyres, they pulled away into the backstreets of Johannesburg.

Back in the stadium, all hell was breaking loose.

Vusi was knocked to the ground as the police tried to follow Charlie across the pitch. Andy and Faya stood in their way next. In his best Scottish brogue, McGeechan sneered something utterly corny like: "Thou shalt not pass." Merv joined them, then The Prof and, one by one, the Royals and the Chiefs blocked the path of the increasingly angry policemen.

Dlamini opened his velvet bag on the grass behind them. Bones and trinkets spilled out. He said a few words. The great cumulo-nimbus crowds that had been building all day suddenly unleashed a rare autumn thunder storm. Huge drops of rain followed by hailstones the size of golf balls rattled down on the warring parties. Everyone ran for the tunnel, the struggle forgotten. Charlie, Sophie, Jabu junior and little Lilly were safely away.

By now, the little gang had new wheels. They were in the back of a huge removals van. Hidden behind a wall of heavyweight oak cupboards, they were sat in comfy chairs as the van careered away from Egoli, past the great mine dumps, out into the Highveld and towards the mountains and the sea. Twice they were stopped. The back doors opened, the police looked inside the cupboards, the twins kept miraculously quiet, the search ended.

Charlie and his three dependants cuddled up in a huge armchair. They slept. And talked. The hours passed. A smell of petrol at the next stop. Drinks and sandwiches appeared from the cab through a tiny hatch. An apparently endless journey ended with a lurch. Still in his green No10 shirt, Charlie led them out when the big back doors were finally opened by the driver... Nkosana Poti with his stitch-ridden nose.

East London, a port two hours north of Port Elizabeth, lay outside bathed in early morning light. They had been travelling all night. Nkosana talked quickly as they crossed the dock to a small speed boat. "This is how we sometimes get our worst criminals out of the country," he grinned, "Travel well. Good luck, all of you."

They hugged Nkosana and clambered into the speed boat. The twins loved it as they swept out to a tanker standing off the harbour.

The captain, a big Greek fellow, welcomed them, showed them to remarkably comfortable quarters, deep inside his enormous, odour-rich craft. They were safe. The engines growled and, within the hour, South Africa began to fall away in the distance. They had escaped. A miracle. Back in the port, Nkosana spotted two unmarked cars following him. A night in the cells would follow. And more pain. New scars.

CHAPTER 10: RIGHT

"The thorn in your foot is temporarily appeased. But it is still in"
Longo proverb (Tanzania)

They landed two weeks later in Southampton. Their time on the Greek tanker *Oddysea* had been curiously satisfying. Comfortable quarters, good food, great weather. Charlie, who often suffered from sea-sickness on trips across the channel as a boy, was right as rain. The tanker had a rough-and-ready gym and a circuit of the vast ship's perimeter provided an adequate running track to keep a level of fitness and provide a distraction from the long days at sea. The kids were spoiled by all the crew, Sophie was initially a subject only of lust among the seamen but, as always, she had soon become an unimpeachable sounding board for everyone's domestic problems by the time they docked amid tumultuous farewells from captain and crew.

But if their time on board ship had been surprising, the welcome in England was staggering. Jabu had been busy. There was a delegation of ANC officials from London, a gaggle of journalists – including Dunnie from his local paper and Neil Harris from the Mail – plus his mum, clearly the worse for wear. Oh, and three immigration officers.

Talking had already taken place between the ANC and the British government. Sophie and the twins, without passports, were given immediate refugee status. Adoption papers were drawn up and signed on the spot. The ANC guys and the journalists filled Charlie and Sophie in on the fall-out from the resettlement camp story.

The BBC and the NBC had both sent war-hardened camera crews to find and film the burned out clinic and other, similar sites in the Ciskei and further afield where the dead and dying lay, forgotten. The South Africans had tried to argue their way out of it, ignore the furore, but eventually they agreed, publicly, to suspend their resettlement program and slow the rush to repatriate unemployed South Africans to the undeveloped homelands.

And Charlie's post-final interview, detailing the Trojan Horse incident, had been backed up too, by other eye-witnesses in other townships around the country. Again, the South African government had been shamed into some sort of promise that such tactics would never be used again.

They broke those promises. For the next five years, rather than easing up, the National Party simply tried to bludgeon the black opposition into submission. A state of emergency was declared, hundreds more died or disappeared. And the demonstrations at Trafalgar Square grew in size and intensity, with Charlie and Sophie occasionally travelling up to join in. Both feared for the future of South Africa, for the well-being of those they had left behind.

Charlie struggled to put his brief stay in South Africa into perspective. He had seen so much in three short months, been through such an emotional roller-coaster, he could hardly believe it. He had to feel the scar on the back of his head to remind him of his first goal in Umlazi. Touch the nick in his ear to recall the first night he had met Sophie and the police had fired on them. But he needed no reminding of the Trojan Horse incident... or the Ciskei. Both would be forever etched in his memory, a source of endless night terrors.

But there were plenty of other things to do. Jabu junior and little Lilly, rapidly approaching five, were sent to school in Lee-on-the-Solent, in a small state primary accustomed to taking Ghanaian, West Indian and Asian children with parents in the navy. Integration was not always easy – Jabu was a handful at the best of times – but both twins were soon at the top of the class on most fronts.

They lived in the little village opposite the Isle of Wight, famous for launching the first hovercraft, and Sophie found herself a job at Portsmouth Football Club, with a little help from Dunnie. The initial mistrust and shock at finding a black South African running the marketing side of the once-great club caused a few problems. But Sophie being Sophie, soon convinced all and sundry that she could cope with managers, directors, supporters, footballers, advertisers and community representatives. Even journalists. She treated them all the same. Firm but fair. And nobody got the better of her.

It was Charlie who struggled. His mother was in bad shape. Her son's appearance in the headlines - for his football and his African horror stories – encouraged her to try to sell her story to the tabloids. It didn't go well. She was eventually rejected even by the News of the World. She died soon afterwards, her liver wrecked, her life a mess. It was a tough time for Charlie, who was still coming to terms with his experiences in Africa.

Initially, Charlie's impressive record for the Chaka Royals – 17 goals and two trophies in nine games - opened doors. He was signed by Southampton and thrived in the reserves. His first team debut came against Millwall at the dangerous Den.

Unlike the rest of the team, they had gone up early to London to demonstrate outside the embassy. He turned up with Sophie and the twins on the train with the fans. The road to the stadium was marked by racist remarks and, as they got closer to the ground, he was recognised as "that bloke who helped the Zulus" and he found himself firmly on the other side of the racial fence. With his Zulu wife and Xhosa children, he was now re-classified as black in the eyes of the Millwall fans. They got in the ground safely, met up with the squad. But he was roundly abused from the kick-off. Monkey chants, bananas on the pitch, absolute filth even from the kids at the front of the terraces.

Charlie tried to take it in his stride. He hit a post and made the Saints' only goal in a 1-1 draw, earning a decent review from most of the football writers. But it made him sick inside that he had to confront raw racism here, in England, the land he had held up to all those in South Africa as a nation free of such things.

It wasn't of course. The four of them were constantly subjected to jibes and put-downs. Charlie had always been considered "a bit dark", now he was black, given his marriage to a "native". On particularly bad days, he even thought about getting Dlamini over to dye his hair beach-blond again.

Fortunately the boots could still talk for him. Charlie enjoyed two good seasons in the top flight, scoring goals but generally moving back into the hole just behind the strikers, a role he had gravitated towards late in his South African safari. He stayed in touch with Jabu and Roy Wegerle, who came over, initially with Chelsea, before moving to QPR where he scored the goal of the season on television. Others, like Jon Paskin from Hellenic and Gavin Nebbeling from Arcadia, came over and played for Wolves and Crystal Palace. Later there would be more, with Chiefs exports Lucas Radebe and Philemon Masinga leading the second wave at Leeds United.

Charlie never quite rose to such heights. He came to accept, over the years, that he was a good striker, but not great. He often pondered the role of Dlamini in his brief Royals' heyday. He never scored goals like that again. Never approached that strike rate of nearly two goals a game.

The instincts, the touches, he had enjoyed in that all-too-short spell, never really returned to light up his game.

Okay, the standard was way better in England, but those uncanny prescient moments, strange glimpses of the future... they never came again. Without the muti-soaked ribbon around his midriff, he was just an ordinary player, capable of occasional brilliance, but the magic appeared to have deserted him.

And when he had his knee mangled for the third time while on loan at Gillingham five grim winters after his African adventure, he had to accept his playing days were over.

By now, young black players like Lawrie Cunningham and Viv Anderson were breaking into the England team, but there was no sign of a black manager on the horizon. So Charlie made that his goal. He did all the coaching badges, completed all the refereeing courses and, trading on his high profile in the media where he had been in demand since the day they landed in Southampton, he got the job as assistant reserve manager at Brighton. He was on the ladder.

And all the time of course, he and Sophie pined for Africa. But there was no way they could go back. The state of emergency brought television pictures of necklacing, police informers killed by placing a burning tyre around their necks. The townships were becoming deliberately unmanageable. The army was deployed in the cities rather than on the border. Toy-toying thousands and mass strikes were way too much for the police force. It looked like the country they loved was going to explode.

Until February 11, 1990. The day they released Nelson Rolihlahla Mandela after 27 long years, 18 of them isolated on Robben Island, a tiny dot of land off Cape Town fit only for seals and lonely fishermen.

From there it was, from 5,000 miles away, an incredibly smooth and rapid path to an unexpectedly peaceful revolution. President FW De Klerk had somehow accepted the inevitable and the first open elections took place in 1993. People queued for hours to cast their historic votes. The ANC came to power and Apartheid was officially dead. At least on the statute books. The demonstrations were over. British people – black and white - started to ask Charlie and Sophie about the "Rainbow Nation", about what it would be like to go there, as tourists.

At first they were hesitant, surely it wasn't all over. The pain, the hatred, the disappearances, BOSS, pass books, homelands, signs on the benches. But looking at the television images, reading the newspapers, Charlie and Sophie and their fellow exiles in London were reasonably encouraged. There was plenty of talk about crime, car-jacking and murder... but in a nation of haves and have-nots, that had always been the case.

Under Apartheid, Sophie told her increasingly sophisticated friends, there was plenty of crime. The police and the Nationalists had been responsible for most of it, now the poor were getting their share any way they could.

Then the Peace and Reconciliation Commission began to delve into the past, getting the police and government officials to reveal their crimes, apologise to the families of those who disappeared forever, those who had been shot. The long list of informers was made public, the millions spent on propaganda was revealed. Government departments, like the old Department of Information, had been paying celebrities to be positive about Apartheid. The Department of Transport had been building a network of roads not to help tourists get from Cape Town to Johannesburg, but to allow the South African Defence Force to travel quickly and efficiently to wipe out any signs of revolution.

The reconciliators also talked about the Trojan Horse operation in Athlone in 1985, the uprising in Soweto in 1976, the Sharpeville shootings of 1961. All was laid bare. Murderers met the families of the murdered. Disappearers talked, tearfully, with those they had attempted to disappear. South African government officials admitted to sending bombs in the post, to spying on exiles overseas, to all kinds of indescribable acts. And a cardiologist now known as Dr Death, Wouter Basson, confessed to a leading role in the government's biological and chemical weapons programs, where he helped to develop "toys of death" like the screwdriver modified to deliver a lethal injection in the event of a sudden anti-apartheid outburst.

It was all there, out in the open. And still the Rainbow Nation stayed on track. Mandela was working his magic.

Charlie, while amazed at the transformation in South Africa, travelled far and wide to further his managerial career in football. He appeared regularly on television, analysing African football and dissecting Premiership games live. Utilising bits of what he had learned from Jabu, Clive and even Dlamini (though he never did use a calabash), Charlie rose up through the ranks, managing Slough Town, Dover Athletic and eventually Bournemouth before the FA recognised his talent with youngsters and took him on as National Youth Development coach on a huge salary.

They lived comfortably in the well-to-do corridor along the A3 between London and Portsmouth. Lilly grew into a fine young woman, and after graduation from Oxford, she became Sophie's personal assistant as chief executive at Portsmouth. Jabu struggled in his early teenage years but eventually found himself, like his step-father, coping through football. He was on the books at Portsmouth, played three or four reserve team games at 15 and then the uncle Jabu, watching his videos and using his telephone in Durban, made an official approach.

He wanted Jabu Junior to play for the Royals. As a South African, as was his birth right. It was time to go back. Their trip co-incided with the 1997 Lions tour. The globe had witnessed the coming together of the Rainbow Nation for the 1995 Rugby World Cup, now Charlie, Sophie, Lilly and Jabu joined scores of huge rugby fans on the jumbo jets to Johannesburg. Nobody on the plane was intimidated by a trip to darkest Africa. Most had been before. Thousands of new tourist attractions, mostly game parks, had opened up, the service was good and the accommodation dirt-cheap, and they found themselves being told by the British rugby fans: "It's the best place in the world to visit. Why don't you go more often?"

The nation had indeed changed. The whites lived behind huge fences, every paper was dominated by horrific crime stories and there was a stench of corruption hanging over most of the major government contracts. But Sophie reasoned, once more, that it had always been thus in Africa, the whites were just slicker conmen.

On the streets, things were surprisingly relaxed. Black, coloured, Asian and white all went to restaurants together now, to cinemas, shopping malls and, when they got to Durban, the beachfront was open to all. At last.

The four of them travelled not to KwaMashu but up on to the Berea to meet Jabu after an absence of more than a decade. He hadn't changed a bit. A slightly-stooped Dlamini was living in the "servant's quarters", a high electrical fence kept envious fellow-Zulus at arm's length while Jabu and his three wives lived in luxury with what appeared to be an entire tribe of pint-sized Ntulanis.

The surprise homecoming party was quite something. Nearly all of the Royals double-winning side was there, though Vusi, inevitably, hadn't made it through the worst of the "emergency" years at the end of the 80s. He had simply disappeared. On the other hand, Solomon, long-lost Solomon Phagate the Mercury photographer and aspiring football writer, emerged through the throng to shake the Englishman's hand. Charlie cried his eyes out, like a dam unleashed. For years he'd assumed he had played a part in Solomon's permanent disappearance. But, after six years in jail on Robben Island, he had been released and now co-edited Ilanga. Merv was there, with his Indian girlfriend and a whole new attitude. Andy was rich and comfortable, with his Scottish accent only slightly Africanised. Teenage and Ace were grey but still looked capable of running the 100m in about 12 seconds, even at 50. Henry the goalkeeper still traded on his Royals career and minor film star status, Moses Faya looked fit as a fiddle, Trigger Mulatsi ran a sports shop.

Jabu Junior trained down at the University with a grey-haired

Clive Fox and the new, sleek generation of Royals. Fox – though his various club sides never quite managed another double - had coached South Africa through their first World Cup campaign at France 98, and would probably go back and do it again in the future with a certain Jomo Nkomo. Charlie stood with Andy, Merv and The Prof, who had been Namibia's national coach for a few years, watching his adopted son play. At 16, he had learned to be tough like Charlie, but though there was no blood link, he had The Prof's poise. He possessed a mesmeric, intoxicating talent which struggled to come to the fore in the teak-tough Academy leagues in England.

Here, he was less likely to get his flashing legs broken. He could run free. And he did. The endless hours in the garden and then down at the local Rec had paid off. So had the years of driving him to football on frosty Sunday mornings. Clive and Jabu got their heads together. Jabu Junior would be staying in South Africa to play in the new-look NPL, where games were played during the summer. And he would get the chance to trace his roots among the Xhosa people.

Then there was the marriage ceremony. A decade before Sophie and Charlie had adopted the children and been joined in a civil ceremony. Now it was time for the big Zulu bash, out in the countryside north of Stanger, about an hour up the coast. And years after Dlamini had told him he'd need cattle when he met Sophie, Charlie found himself having to pay traditional African "lobola" for his wife – in the days of Chaka, cows were given to the family of the bride by the husband-to-be. Now it was cash in return for a lavish ceremony, overseen by old "Mad-Eyes" himself.

And Charlie was happy to pay The Prof, who was starting to come over to Britain to visit more and more, pretending to scout for players but probably just keen to be near his "overseas" family.

Charlie, Sophie and Lilly, who had no intention of staying away from her friends in England, returned to Heathrow. There was a sadness but it was tinged with the knowledge Jabu Junior was where he belonged. Scoring goals against Chiefs and Pirates. For Jabu, the teenage years as a black lad in up-market Surrey had been difficult. He explained quietly to his "dad" that he felt at home, finally, after all the years of being different. Lilly felt none of the dislocation. She couldn't believe he didn't want to go "home". And she wasn't too unhappy about becoming the only child for a while. Not all twins come from the same pod.

Sophie and Charlie had tried for children for years before a specialist explained, mystified, that she appeared to have been sterilised. Sophie recalled her appendix being removed when she was 17. It had happened then, she surmised, against her will and without her knowledge in the local hospital. The white doctor had simply been following orders from on high. Together they searched the internet to find out why and how she had been robbed of her right to bear children. And there it was, in electronic black and white, the evidence presented to the Truth and Reconciliation committee telling how sterilisation had been encouraged and eventually linked to AIDS treatment.

Though tough to take, childlessness didn't break them. The lad from Fareham and the princess from KwaZulu had stayed strong. Best friends, ardent lovers and now, after years of moving in powerful circles,

academics. Both of them had taken part-time masters degrees, Sophie in marketing, Charlie in history and politics.

Charlie still gave after-dinner speeches on the horrors of Apartheid and the magic of African football, Sophie gave business seminars and encouraged more women to try working in the male-dominated world of football.

It was no surprise when, with the 2010 World Cup in South Africa coming up, Charlie was made communications director to Flavio Bonetti, England's brilliant Italian coach.

June 11 was the key date. The big kick-off. Africa's first World

Cup. England's first game was scheduled against the United States in Rustenburg two days later. Charlie, Sophie and Lilly travelled with the England squad to their pre-tournament training camp. This was what they had waited all their lives for. A World Cup in a transformed land. Jabu Junior, the orphan from the resettlement camp, had just been appointed captain of the struggling hosts, better known as Bafana Bafana, the Boys, the Boys, the hopeful but lowest ranked home side in the history of the World Cup.

And here we must leave them. Standing watching England train on the bright new training facilities at Bafokeng Sports Palace, hand in hand, the Zulu princess and the Hampshire lad whose dad is from somewhere exotic. The police pass by without a second glance. Lilly is chatting with the fans, black and white, rich and poor, English and African. Not a whiff of tear-gas. No sirens. There are no whites-only benches or Bantu entrances to the hotel behind them. For the next month, colour will count for nothing. It won't matter where your dad was from. Just how good you are, how hard you try. And, perhaps, what you've got in your calabash.

EPILOGUE

"A fish is in water but does not know the importance of water"
Ewe proverb (Ghana, Benin, Nigeria and Togo)

If you drive around Frankfort, a tiny village in the Eastern Cape now, you may still find deep, concreted holes in the ground if you leave the tar roads and search the nearby fields. These remnants of "long-drop" toilets are the only lingering signs of the resettlement camps which once blighted the area. My research suggests the shanty I chanced upon as a student in 1981 was called Umgwali, though I'm still not sure.

If you google "sterilisation", "South African Bureau of State Security", "Trojan Horse" and/or "Dr Wouter Basson" you can find similar shards of a history which would be best off deep in a toilet and left, for reasons of sanity rather than sanitation, to rot away.

As a young journalist and footballer, I didn't go into the townships to lay bare a tyrannical political system or to publicise the behaviour of a police force careering out of control. I went to write about and play football. To show off the length of my throw-in, my ability in the air (but not quick feet or spectacular ball control). Like any other youngster. But to ignore what I saw around me would have been impossible. As a result I spent several nights in squalid cells, had my phone bugged and found myself followed home a couple of times before I eventually fled back to London in 1985. Nearly 25 years ago. Time should erode the memories, democracy has eased the inequalities, the newspaper cuttings are yellow and slightly curly.

But to forget Apartheid, the grand plan dreamt up by Dutch-born president HF Verwoerd and his cronies, would be a crime. To pretend his legions of willing accomplices – academics, politicians, policemen, secret agents, scientists, historians and ordinary folk - didn't exist would be wrong. A 2009 visit to the Apartheid Museum just outside Johannesburg helps keep the memories sharp, though in many ways the whole thing is too soft. A couple of old Afrikaners talking on grainy videos about the "barbarian Bantu" they needed to control; a few benches with faded "Europeans Only" signs; the life story of Nelson Mandela; intelligent, earnest guides. They all count, they all help.

But the true misery of South Africa before 1993 can only be appreciated by those who lived there. Not in the middle class white homes with swimming pools like my parents. In the townships, the shanty towns, the slums. In resettlement camps like Crossroads, the rotting shack city which replaced the lively hub of District Six before another wave of bulldozers came.

European visitors to South Africa in the new Millennium may be disturbed by the stories of rampant crime which dominate the press. Just six months before the big kick-off, the security company looking after the German team at the World Cup in South Africa suggested the players should only leave their hotel in bullet-proof vests. Brilliant. Typical of the European approach to the new South Africa. That rampant paranoia is weakening, but still prevalent. Europe likes to see post-colonial Africa as the dark continent. Dangerous, dirty, demonic. It's hard to shake the old routine.

The truth is of course, South Africa is a modern miracle, a lasting monument to man's capacity to forgive. And, if you stick to the tar roads, a great place to go on holiday.

If you visit the Rainbow Nation over the next couple of years after reading this book – whether it's to attend the World Cup, see the incredible game parks, follow a cricket or rugby tour, to shop in Sandton where prices remain incredibly cheap or simply to bask on the beautiful beaches (God, now it sounds like a tourism guide) – try to remember how it really was for the vast majority of people down near the tip of Africa.

No vote, no voice. No unemployment benefit, no National Health Service. Just grinding poverty and the prospect of resettlement if you were picked up without a stamped pass book. Oh, and if you were a woman, the risk of being sterilised while the doctor offered a routine medical examination. That particular gem, passed on by a National Serviceman forced to tend to the local populace in his uniform, has never been forgotten.

No, this stuff is not the product of a fertile imagination, enhanced by years of comfortable living in Britain. It's history. Fact. And best none of us forget it.

UPDATE FROM THE AUTHOR

January 2010

ILLOVO, JOHANNESBURG: I've been here a month now, yet another return to Africa. Since mid-December I've been covering the four-match Test series between England and South Africa. It's been an incredible struggle on the cricket field.

But like all sport, what happens off the field is integral to the experience. I've been to Centurion, just outside Pretoria, Durban, Cape Town and now Johannesburg.

Four entirely different cities, these are the four major World Cup venues later in the year. I attended a game between the local Premier League champions Supersport United and rock-bottom Jomo Cosmos at Loftus Versfeld, the World Cup stadium in the South African administrative capital, Pretoria.

It's where hosts South Africa will play Uruguay on June 16 and the USA take on Algeria on June 23, just two of the five qualifying games scheduled for the 50,000-capacity rugby stadium opened in 1903 and refurbished many times, the last in 2008.

I was one of the few white fans in evidence, but there was no sense of insecurity or differentness. An electrician called Reggie took me under his wing and gave me a run down on the state of local football. He even offered a tour of the townships and a trip to see the great Kaizer Chiefs. Afterwards, dressed in an England football jersey, I was hugged by the Supersport fans outside as they celebrated a 3-0 victory. "We'll beat you at the World Cup," they laughed, hopefully.

Outside the scenic Centurion cricket ground, the brand new Gautrain rail link flies on concrete stilts through the air over the motorways. Most of it will be open in time for the big kick-off on June 11. It is a major feat of modern engineering and a major drain on any nation's resources, costing billions.

And everywhere in Centurion, the rapidly growing metropolis north of Pretoria, there is an awareness the world is coming to town. What can I tell you? That the Velmore Estate, just outside the tiny suburb of Erasmia, will house Michael Ballack and the German team? Magnificent place. Google it. Remote, backing on to the tranquil Hennops River. Helpful staff showed my father and I around the spa, an oxygen chamber and luxury rooms, complex medical facilities – they're even building a poolside beach.

In Centurion itself, the Italians will be at Leriba Lodge and the Americans will go to Irene Lodge, a mile away. Beautiful African venues with lakes and traditional thatch in evidence. Both will train at local high schools, where special pitches have been laid for the international onslaught of football studs training at altitude, preparing for a World Cup a different heights, but blissfully free of Apartheid.

In neighbouring Pretoria, Diego Maradona's Argentina will be based at the University's High Performance Centre, where the trans-sexual world athletics champion Caster Semenya was coaxed to stardom.

Then, in Muldersdrift, one step closer to Johannesburg, the Australians are staying at beautiful Kloofsicht in the middle of nowhere while the Dutch have chosen the centre of opulent Joburg suburb Sandton for their base, training at the Milpark Stadium, home of local side Wits.

And I even discovered the England training camp outside

Rustenburg. Secret, luxurious, not complete until May. Built by the Bafokeng tribe, who earn a percentage from the numerous local platinum mines, the Bafokeng Sports Palace complex offers 17 grass pitches, five artificial surfaces, swimming pools and a magnificent low-slung hotel complex fit for a king. King Kagosi Leruo Molotgeti to be precise. The local monarch has been heavily involved in the project which will become the highest altitude training camp in the country.

The first British journalist to enter the facility, I finally found the burgeoning complex under construction behind a fading motel facade six kilometres along the road to Africa's Las Vegas Sun City from the Bafokeng World Cup stadium in underdeveloped Phokeng (mind how you pronounce that).

Just by chance (the World Cup draw on December 4 last year was very kind to them!) England will open their campaign against the USA there on June 12 in front of a full-house 42,000 fans from the two best supported nations in South Africa. And they'll be back for their first knock-out game in the same magnificent bowl if they win Group C. You can read more about this – and see exclusive photographs - on my website at www.nealcollins.co.uk.

Then on to the Boxing Day Test in Durban, another town undergoing huge World Cup construction. There I visited the magnificent new Moses Mabhida Stadium, which will host five qualifiers and a semi-final. A magnificent arched arena right next to the huge King's Park rugby stadium, it will hold 70,000 and they are just finishing the construction of a fans' walkway to nearby Battery Beach.

Already fans are able to take a cablecar over the arch and they are even planning to allow bungy jumping from the highest point. Incredible!

Durban is a vast, cosmopolitan port, shared by Europeans, Asians and Zulus. I walked to the beach from the luxurious Hilton Hotel a mile away and felt completely at home on the African seaside, body surfing in the huge rollers of the Indian Ocean, where once black people were banned from bathing.

New Year took us to Cape Town and another brand new stadium at Green Point. The scenery has to be seen to be believed. Nestled under Signal Hill next to the landmark Table Mountain, the parliamentary capital of South Africa is another cosmopolitan port, where all colours, all creeds, are now free to mingle.

My wife Tracy and I walked the main road – Long Street – at 2am on New Year's night amid the revellers. And despite her alarmingly short evening dress, we only received hearty "Happy New Years" from the teeming masses. It was an evening that capped a very moving return to Africa.

And finally, as I write, I find myself in Johannesburg at the plush Wanderers Protea hotel. Two World Cup stadiums here. Ellis Park, the nation's historic rugby stadium which can hold 62,000 after recent refurbishment. First used in 1926, the venue where South Africa won the nation-unifying Rugby World Cup in 1995 will host five qualifiers and a quarter-final.

Then, on the other side of the city near the fabled township of Soweto where the seeds of freedom were sown in 1976, we have Soccer City. A crowd of 94,700 will fill the Kalabash-shaped (cauldron-shaped) stadium for the opening game of the World Cup between the hosts and Mexico. It will also be the venue for the final on June 11. What a day that promises to be.

Johannesburg is the most troubled of South Africa's cities. It's always been a fascinating hotchpotch, since the Witwatersrand gold rush of the 19th century brought fortune hunters from around the world to the heart of Africa.

Today it is a bustling metropolis, the biggest city in South Africa and still the commercial capital, where it all happens, where the stock exchange keeps this nation ahead of the rest of the continent economically.

There is a third-world fear of crime in the streets here, but only in certain areas, like any major city. I suggest caution, but no need for rampant paranoia.

For four weeks, with thousands of English "Barmy Army" cricket fans, we have traversed the nation, discovering new gems, shrugging off the xenophobia of the European media which suggests we must always be on our guard in post-Apartheid South Africa.

And everywhere the changes wrought in 16 years of democracy are evident. Find me a nation which has developed more than this one since 1993. The 35-mile stretch between Pretoria and Johannesburg has mushroomed beyond belief.

Once there were miles of empty bushveld between the cities. Now Centurion, Midrand and Sandton are joined by thousands of middle class homes, shopping malls and retail outlets. This is boom time, even in a recession.

Rustenburg has grown beyond recognition, as have three further World Cup cities, Port Elizabeth, Nelspruit and Polokwane. Game Parks abound. When the nation changed there were around 60 safari parks. Now there are over 6,000. Take time when you visit, make sure you take a dawn or dusk game drive. You'll never forget it.

Durban has rebuilt the once-troubled Point Road area south of the city, creating an African paradise called Ushaka, all restaurants, aquariums and shops. At one venue, built in a ship wreck, you eat lobster watched by sharks in a two-storey high glass tank at your elbow.

Up the north coast, tiny villages like Umdhloti and Ballito have become major resorts. Umhlanga offers the biggest shopping centre in the southern hemisphere.

And they've got the new runway near La Mercy opening in March, so two airports will ferry the thousands of football fans into the city, from the industrial south and the sugar-cane festooned north.

And in Cape Town, the jewel at the tip of Africa, growth along the waterfront, where former prisoners host boat trips to Nelson Mandela's now-defunct political jail on Robben Island, continues unfettered by the global economic downturn.

In one day, we saw the seals at Hout Bay, the penguins at Boulder Beach and baboons at Cape Point where the Atlantic and Indian Oceans meet. We travelled by cable car up the mountain, by funicular railway to the Cape Point lighthouse, by coach around the magnificent Chapman's Peak.

I've already been on 702 radio here talking about the upcoming tournament, Africa's first World Cup. Explaining that so much of what the Rainbow Nation has achieved since 1993 should be considered nearly miraculous. This is the start of my World Cup crusade.

Surprisingly, there is positive feedback - even from the staunch Afrikaners, who had their hard-won political power torn away by the surprise Nelson Mandela/FW De Klerk double act in the early 1990s.

For over 40 years, Apartheid was shoved down the throats of every young white man in South Africa. We are the master race, they were told, at school and in church, at home and at work.

For over 40 years, the indigenous folk were told they were the foreigners here, second class citizens in their own land, at school and in church, at home and at work.

But South Africa today is the Rainbow Nation. A black middle class has emerged from nowhere. Articulate Africans abound, defying years of poorly funded "Bantu Education". Black and white eat together, worship together, live together. It seems like yesterday they couldn't even share a bench together.

Over the last month, thousands of English cricket fans and

international tourists will have seen what I have witnessed. An African nation emerging as a world force, a colour blind Rainbow Nation capable of miracles.

And soon the world will see it. Every television, every newspaper will focus on Africa's first World Cup from June 11 to July 11. And I hope they see what we've seen.

If you enjoyed the book, you can keep up with the author's sporting adventures at www.nealcollins.co.uk/blog